"So what do you think ... ... you come?

Cooper let out a long breath. "I don't know, Kate," she said. "You know I'm done with all of that."

"I know," Kate said, "but this isn't really like doing something with a lot of people. It's just me and Annie."

"I just don't think I'd be any use," Cooper said. "You know you have to be in the right frame of mind for this stuff to work right. I don't want to bring any negative energy to it."

There was more silence as Kate didn't respond. Then she said, "The three of us have done some really great work together. Your energy was part of that. In fact, if it weren't for you we would proba-bly never have gotten together."

"That was different," Cooper protested. "I was really into all of it then. I'm not now. I know you and Annie don't understand what happened to me, but it wasn't a lot of fun. I don't want to get involved with that kind of thing again."

Follow the Circle:

circle of three

BOOK
6

Ring of Light

Isobel Bird

AVON BOOKS

An Imprint of HarperCollins*Publishers*

CHAPTER I

"Come on," Kate said, grabbing Tyler's hand and pulling him up the front walk to her house. "It's not going to be that bad."

"Easy for you to say," Tyler joked as he followed along behind her. "You're not the one spending the day with your girlfriend's parents for the first time."

Kate stopped at the door and turned to look at her boyfriend. His black hair was, as usual, tousled but adorable, and his eyes, a peculiar deep gold color, sparkled in the July sun. Her parents had met Tyler a few times and seemed to like him, but she was still a little nervous. This was the first time they'd all be together for more than half an hour. Tyler was the first guy she'd brought home since Scott, and they'd thought that Scott was the perfect boyfriend for her. They hadn't understood when she broke things off with him, and she knew that might make them particularly critical of Tyler, who had replaced Scott as the guy in her life.

"Don't worry," she said, reassuring herself as

much as she was reassuring Tyler. "They're going to *love* you."

Tyler grinned. "That would be nice," he said, "but the only one I need to love me is you."

Kate rolled her eyes, but inside she was thrilled to hear Tyler say that. Only recently had either of them said the L-word, and it was still new to her. Every time Tyler said it, she felt like she was the most important person in the world.

"I do love you," she said, leaning up and kissing him.

Just as their lips met, the front door opened and her father's face appeared.

"Am I interrupting something?" he said gruffly.

Startled, Kate pulled away from her boyfriend and instinctively wiped her hand across her mouth in embarrassment.

"Hi, Daddy," she said, trying to keep her composure.

"Hello, Mr. Morgan," Tyler said, doing a much better job than Kate was of pretending that they hadn't just been caught making out. "It's nice to see you again."

Mr. Morgan reached out and took Tyler's offered hand, shaking it firmly while looking his daughter's boyfriend up and down carefully. "Nice to see you again, too," he said evenly.

Avoiding her father's gaze, Kate slipped past him and into the house, drawing Tyler after her. She hustled him through the living room and into the kitchen, where her mother was rushing around doing ten different things at once as she prepared the food for the cookout they were having.

"Hi, honey," Mrs. Morgan said as she turned from checking something in the oven and went back to chopping celery at the counter.

When she saw Tyler standing behind her daughter she stopped what she was doing and smiled at him. "Hi, Tyler," she said. "I'd shake hands but I'm afraid they're covered in barbeque sauce, flour, and who knows what else."

"That's okay," Tyler said. "I get the idea, and whatever it is you're cooking, it smells amazing, so the trade-off is more than worth it."

Mrs. Morgan looked at Kate. "This one's a flatterer," she said. "Watch out for those. They'll get you every time. I should know—it's how your father got me."

Kate blushed. "Well, everything does smell great," she said, trying to change the subject. "What's on the menu?"

"The usual Fourth of July picnic spread," her mother replied. "Hot dogs, fried chicken, corn on the cob, potato salad, baked beans, and chocolate cake."

"I smell something else," Kate said, sniffing the air around the oven. She opened the door and peeked inside, where she saw a pan of lasagna sitting on one of the racks.

"Lasagna?" she said suspiciously. "You only make lasagna when—"

"When Kyle's home?" a voice behind her finished.

Kate wheeled around, letting out a squeal of surprise when she saw her older brother standing there, a huge grin on his face and his arms held open. She ran to him and wrapped her arms around him as he picked her up and swung her around.

"What are you doing here?" she asked when he finally put her down. "I thought you were staying at the university this summer to work."

"I am," Kyle said. "But I have a little time off. Besides, I had to bring you something."

"Bring me something?" Kate said. "What do you mean?"

"Oh, it's just a little present I picked up on the way here," Kyle answered mysteriously. "Want to see it? It's out back."

Kate looked at her mother, who was also now grinning wickedly.

"Do you know about this?" Kate asked her.

"You'll just have to go and see for yourself," her mother said, pretending to be busy ripping up lettuce for a salad.

Kate headed for the back door with everyone following behind her. She had no idea what Kyle could be talking about. It wasn't her birthday or anything, and she was surprised enough to see him home for the Fourth. What else could he have brought with him?

She burst through the screen door and stepped

into the backyard, looking around for her big surprise. What she saw was the barbeque, the coals already glowing, and a picnic table piled with paper plates and plastic utensils. Then she noticed that someone was sitting in one of the lawn chairs that had been set out. When she realized who it was, she gasped.

"Aunt Netty?" she said, not believing her eyes.

"The one and only," said the woman in the chair as she stood up. "Surprised?"

Kate darted forward and hugged her aunt tightly, all the while laughing with delight. She couldn't believe it—her favorite aunt was standing in her backyard.

"I told you I picked up something you would like," Kyle said teasingly.

Kate turned to Tyler, who was standing in the doorway silently watching the goings-on. "This is my Aunt Netty," she said happily.

"I got that part," Tyler quipped. He stepped forward and shook the woman's hand. "I'm Tyler," he told her.

Aunt Netty raised an eyebrow and turned to her niece. "Not bad at all," she said. "I see you inherited the Rampling women's good taste in men."

She turned back to Tyler and smiled. "Don't take me too seriously," she said. "I'm just teasing."

"No problem," Tyler responded. "I happen to think Kate has pretty good taste in men myself."

Everyone laughed at his joke. Kate, who still

hadn't let go of her aunt's hand, was looking at her closely. "You cut your hair," she said. "It used to hang down past your shoulders."

Aunt Netty shook her head. She was wearing a straw hat, and her hair barely touched her shoulders. "I didn't like all of that hair hanging in my face," she said. "Do you like the new look? I think it's kind of Audrey Hepburn in *Breakfast at Tiffany's*."

"Sure," Kate answered. "Now, tell me how long you're here for. I suppose it's just for the weekend, right?"

"That's the best part of the surprise," her aunt said. "I'm here for a longer visit this time."

Kate couldn't believe her good luck. Not only was her favorite aunt there, she was going to stay for a while. "A week?" she asked hopefully.

"At least," said her aunt. "It depends on how things go with the project I'm working on."

"This is so great," Kate exclaimed. "What better way to spend the Fourth of July than with my favorite people?"

"How about *eating* with your favorite people?" her father suggested as he came out with a platter piled high with hot dogs and headed for the grill. "I think your mother could use a hand bringing the rest of that food out here."

"Let's go make ourselves useful," Aunt Netty suggested to Kate.

"You just sit down, Netty," Mr. Morgan said. "The kids can help Teresa."

Aunt Netty groaned and made a face at Kate's father. "Whatever you say, Joe," she said, and sank back into the lawn chair.

Kate went back into the kitchen, taking Tyler with her. Inside, she loaded him up with things to carry, all the while talking about her aunt.

"She's my mom's little sister," she informed him as she handed him a big bowl of chips. "She's really funny, and she's a photographer. She's always going somewhere different to shoot for magazines. Wait until you see her stuff. She must be here on some kind of assignment."

"She seems really nice," Tyler said, trying to juggle all the things Kate was handing him.

"You can make more than one trip, you know," her mother said.

"Sorry," said Kate, realizing that she'd over-loaded her boyfriend and taking back the napkins she'd tried to squeeze under his arm. "I'm just so excited about Aunt Netty being here."

They went back outside, where Tyler helped Kate arrange things on the picnic table. When everything was ready, the whole family gathered around and began loading up their plates. Mr. Morgan stood by the grill, turning hot dogs and handing them out when they were done. Before long everyone was sitting in lawn chairs, happily eating and enjoying the beautiful sunny afternoon.

"This sure beats cafeteria food," Kyle said as he dug into his second piece of lasagna. "I think the university should hire you to cater for us, Mom."

"Your mother has enough business here to keep her working overtime," Mr. Morgan commented. "Don't give her any ideas. We hardly see her as it is."

"This really is amazing, Mrs. Morgan," Tyler said as he nibbled on an ear of corn. "I can't wait to try some of that cake."

"Do you want some potato salad, Aunt Netty?" Kate asked, glancing at her aunt's plate. "You haven't eaten very much."

"Thanks, sweetie," Aunt Netty replied. "I'm all set. It's all delicious, but like Tyler I'm trying to save room for that cake."

"That just means there's more for me," Kate said, getting up to refill her plate.

"So, Tyler, tell me about yourself," said Kate's aunt when Kate returned and settled back into her seat beside her boyfriend. "Where did you and Kate meet?"

Kate felt herself tense up a little as she waited for Tyler to answer. The truth was that they had met through a Wicca study group she was part of that was run by some members of the coven to which Tyler and his mother belonged. But Kate's family didn't know anything about her interest in witchcraft, and she wasn't ready for them to know about it yet. They were rather conservative. She knew they wouldn't understand what Wicca was all about, and she wasn't sure she was ready to explain it to them. Although she hated keeping secrets from her family, she knew that this was one thing she had to keep under wraps, at least for the time being.

Tyler, on the other hand, had been raised in Wicca. Apart from his father, who was divorced from Tyler's mother and didn't share her views on the Craft, everyone in his life was familiar with Wicca and understood his involvement in it. While Kate wished that she could be open about what she was doing, the fact was that she had to attend the study group in secret. Although this hadn't really been a problem so far, now that she was dating Tyler and had introduced him to her family, the issue was something she thought about more and more. But a Fourth of July picnic was not the place to be giving them that kind of news.

Fortunately, she and Tyler had agreed on an answer to the question they knew was bound to be asked at some point. "We met in a bookstore," Tyler told Aunt Netty.

While technically this wasn't true—they had first met at a ritual for the Spring Equinox—the Wicca study group *was* held at Crones' Circle, a bookstore, and Kate and Tyler *did* meet there every week, so it wasn't entirely a lie.

"A bookstore?" Aunt Netty said. "How romantic. I didn't think there were any men left who read books."

"Hey," Kyle exclaimed. "We're not all dumb, you know."

Aunt Netty patted her nephew's hand. "I know *you* aren't, honey," she said. "But you have to admit that most of your fellow men generally aren't running around in bookstores."

"Tyler reads a lot," Kate said. "More than I do."

"What about sports?" Aunt Netty asked. "Do you play any, Tyler?"

"Not really," Tyler answered. "At least not any team ones. I'm afraid I'm not coordinated enough for that. But I like to run."

Mr. Morgan made a muffled grunt, but he didn't say anything. Kate felt a twinge of resentment at his behavior. She knew he would have preferred it if Tyler were a jock. After all, her father did run a sporting goods store. He had liked the fact that Scott had been the captain of the football team. It had given the two of them something to talk about. But he and Tyler had less in common, and she knew that might make things a little harder for them.

"I think a smart guy is sexier than an athlete any day," Aunt Netty said, catching Kate's eye and winking. "Muscles come and go, but a good mind is a rare thing."

Kate giggled. Leave it to her aunt to always say exactly the right thing to lighten the moment.

"What about you, Aunt Netty?" she asked. "Any men in your life these days?"

"Oh, you know how it is," Netty replied, waving her hand in the air. "They come and they go. I can't keep track of them all."

"Kate," her mother said. "Don't ask such personal questions."

"It's okay, Teresa," Netty said. "After all, I've been grilling the poor girl about *her* love life. She's entitled to one personal question. And the answer is no—I'm between significant others at the moment."

Kate laughed again. Seeing her aunt there, smiling and having a good time, made her happy. It was a great way to celebrate the beginning of summer, and she was glad that Tyler could be there to enjoy it with her.

"How come Cooper and Annie didn't come?" her mother asked her. "Didn't you invite them?"

Suddenly a little of the happiness went out of Kate's afternoon. She cleared her throat. "I invited them," she said. "But they both already had plans with their families."

It was true—Annie and Cooper were both spending the Fourth with their families. At least Kate knew Annie was. She didn't really know what Cooper was doing, and she hadn't really invited her to the cookout. Even thinking about Cooper was hard right now after what had happened a few weeks before.

"Are these the two friends I've heard you talk about?" Aunt Netty asked.

Kate nodded. More than anything she would have liked her two best friends to meet her favorite aunt. But Cooper had decided to stop studying

Wicca. Although Annie and Kate respected her decision, there was no denying that it had changed their friendship. Kate still didn't know exactly what had happened to Cooper on Midsummer Eve, when they all had been running around in the woods at the big ritual they'd attended, but whatever it was had turned Cooper off Wicca, maybe for good. Where before the three of them had talked almost constantly about witchcraft and their respective experiences with learning about it, now Cooper didn't talk to them at all, or at least she hadn't since they'd returned from the trip to the woods. At first Kate and Annie had wanted to give her some space to deal with whatever she was dealing with, assuming she would call them after a few days. But she hadn't, and they weren't sure where Cooper stood on the subject of Wicca—or their friendship.

"I'm sure you'll meet them while you're here," Tyler said, and Kate shot him a look of thanks. Once again she had deflected a potentially difficult conversation with his help.

"I certainly hope so," Aunt Netty said. "Any friends of Kate are sure to be interesting."

The rest of the afternoon passed pleasantly, filled with more eating and then the dull routine of helping Mrs. Morgan clean everything up. Tyler helped Kate wash up, and then they returned to the backyard. As the sun set and the sky turned dark, Kate found herself looking forward excitedly to the centerpiece of the day's festivities—the fireworks.

A few minutes after night fell the first bright splash of color exploded across the sky, sending a rain of golden stars down toward them. Kate sat on the picnic table beside Tyler, watching happily as more and more rockets were sent whistling into the air, where they erupted in fountains of red, blue, and white. The echoes of their explosions filled her ears, and she oohed and aahed along with everyone else as the display of lights grew more and more elaborate.

Kate reached out and took Tyler's hand in hers, feeling his fingers close around her own. She leaned into him, feeling the warmth of him beside her, and she was filled with happiness. Despite what was happening with Cooper, she was excited about the summer that lay ahead. Things were working out in her life, and she had learned that she could handle whatever came her way.

Besides, she was going to get to spend some real quality time with her aunt. That alone was enough to make her whole summer. Added to everything else, it made her feel like the luckiest girl in the world.

She looked around for her aunt and was surprised to discover that she wasn't there. The chair she'd been sitting in was empty. Then she looked around and saw a figure standing in the kitchen, her outline silhouetted in the window.

"I'll be right back," Kate whispered to Tyler, and slipped off the table.

She walked to the back door and went inside. Her aunt was leaning against the sink. She held a glass of water in her hand, and she had just put something into her mouth. She took a sip of water and threw her head back, swallowing. When she looked up and saw Kate there, she quickly put down the glass, picked up a small bottle from the counter, and tucked the bottle into her pocket.

"Hey there," she said. "I didn't hear you come in."

"I just wanted to tell you that you're missing the best part of the show," Kate said.

"I was just coming out," Aunt Netty said. "I just needed to take some aspirin."

"Are you okay?" Kate asked, concerned. "You look a little tired."

"I'm fine," her aunt said. "I just have a headache from being in the sun so long. I'll be okay in a minute. Why don't we go back outside? I bet that boyfriend of yours is missing you."

She put her arm around her niece. Then, suddenly, she hugged Kate tightly. "I'm so glad I get to see you again," she said.

"Me, too," Kate answered, hugging her aunt back.

Netty pulled away. "Now, let's go," she said. "I don't want to miss another minute of this night."

CHAPTER 2

"This is where the dirty sheets go," the nurse said to Annie, showing her the large wheeled hamper that sat in the hallway. "You strip them off the beds and put them in here. Replace the old sheets with new ones from this shelf. When you've done a floor you wheel the whole thing down to the laundry room. It's not exactly rocket science."

Annie laughed nervously. She'd only spent two hours inside Shady Hills and already she wanted to leave. Partly it was the smell—the peculiar combination of antiseptic floor wash and overly sweet perfume. The smell was overwhelming. But mostly it was the sadness. Everywhere she went she saw old people. Their lined faces stared at her as she walked past, and she hated seeing them sitting in their wheelchairs or propped up in their uncomfortable-looking mechanical beds, their eyes staring blankly at the fuzzy pictures on their blaring television sets.

Why did you ever volunteer for this? she asked herself for perhaps the hundredth time that morning. But she *had* volunteered, and she was determined to see her commitment through, so she listened to what the nurse, Mrs. Abercrombie, was telling her.

"Mostly they won't talk to you," the older woman said as she walked down the hallway, her white shoes making soft *whap-whap* sounds on the tile floor. "I don't think most of them even know where they are anymore. Your job is just to clean their rooms, straighten things up, and make sure they have what they need. Usually you'll be doing these rounds while they're at physical therapy or in the common room, so you probably won't see many of them anyway."

That's one good thing, Annie thought silently. She really didn't want to see any of the residents. She tried not to peer through the doorways of the rooms they were passing. But she couldn't help it. The figures in the doorways and on the beds were people, not puppets or mannequins. She found herself wondering how they had ended up in Shady Hills. It wasn't like it was a prison or anything. In fact, it seemed pretty nice. But she couldn't help but see the nursing home as a kind of prison. She knew *she* would never want to have to live in it, or in anyplace like it.

"How long have you been working here?" she asked Mrs. Abercrombie.

"Seventeen years," the nurse answered. "Before you were born, right?"

Annie nodded, and the nurse sighed. "You girls

make me feel old," she said. "Pretty soon I'll be sitting in one of these rooms."

"Don't you find it a little depressing?" asked Annie. "I mean, being around this all day and everything."

Mrs. Abercrombie nodded. "Sometimes," she said. "Holidays are particularly bad. But I look at it this way—we're all going to get old, right? One of these days it really could be me in one of these beds. If I ever am, I want someone to treat me nicely. So I try to do the same for the guests here."

Guests, Annie thought. It was a strange word to use for people who were basically waiting to die. But Mrs. Abercrombie spoke about the patients as if they were at some kind of hotel where everything they might want would be provided for them. Annie imagined her leading the old people in games or encouraging them to take advantage of the all-you-can-eat buffet.

"Let me ask you something," Mrs. Abercrombie said. "Why are you here? You could be doing a lot of other things with your summer, so why this?"

Annie paused. Should she tell the nurse the real reason she was at Shady Hills? She wanted to, but she didn't think it was a good idea.

"I think it will look good on my college applications," she said, hoping the nurse wouldn't ask her too much more about it.

Mrs. Abercrombie grunted. "I get it," she said. "Charity work always looks good. Well, I don't really care why you're here as long as you do your work. Promise me you won't skip out after two weeks and that's good enough for me."

"I won't skip out," Annie said. "I promise."

"Okay then," the nurse replied. "Why don't you finish changing the beds on this floor. When you're done, come find me and I'll show you the rest of your exciting duties."

"Sure," said Annie. "Where should I start?"

"This room is as good as any," Mrs. Abercrombie said. "Work your way down this side and then back up the other."

The nurse walked away, leaving Annie outside the room. Annie turned and looked through the doorway. The blinds on the window were down, and the room was dimly lit by the sunlight coming through the slats. But still it was hard to see.

"Hello?" Annie called. "Is anyone there?"

There was no answer. She tried again, but still no one responded. *Good*, she thought as she went inside. *At least I won't have to talk to anyone.*

She flipped on the light and looked around. Like all of the rooms at Shady Hills, the one she was in was small. The walls had been painted a pale yellow, and on the floor beside the bed was a small yellow rug. Even the curtains were yellow, as if someone thought that surrounding the room's owner with the cheerful color would make the place seem more comforting. It reminded Annie of the classroom she'd had in kindergarten. *I guess they think old people and children both like bright colors*, she mused as she went to the bed and pulled off the bedspread, which was the same shade as everything else.

She pulled the sheets from the bed, wadded them up, and carried them back into the hallway, where she dumped them into the waiting hamper. Taking fresh sheets from the shelf on the side of the cart, she went back and spread the bottom sheet over the mattress. Then came the top sheet, the corners of which she tucked in like her aunt had taught her to do to make them nice and neat. The whole process took only a couple of minutes, and then she was putting the bedspread back over the top.

She started to leave, anxious to get on to the next room. But as she passed the dresser that sat at the foot of the bed, she happened to glance at the items sitting on top of it. There, next to a container of powder and several little vials of medications, was a picture. It showed an old woman surrounded by four smiling young people. The woman was holding a balloon, and behind her there was a big banner reading "Happy Birthday, Grandma!" in big red letters.

Annie looked at the woman's face. Was this her room? Were those her grandchildren? She looked more closely at the picture. While the children were laughing and happy, the woman seemed sad. The hand holding the balloon sat limply in her lap, almost as if the woman didn't know she was holding anything. She looked tired, and Annie felt bad for her.

Annie picked up one of the plastic bottles of pills that sat beside the photograph and looked at the label. "Addie Miller," she read. Was that the woman's name? She figured it must be. Part of her liked knowing that. But another part of her didn't like knowing the real person who lived in that room, who spent every day of her life surrounded by yellow things, looking at a picture of herself holding a balloon.

Annie put down the pills and left the room before she saw anything else. She didn't want to know too much about the people in the home. *But isn't that why you really came here?* she asked herself as she pushed the hamper toward the next room and went inside. *Don't you want to see what it means to grow old? Didn't you decide to do this after your night with the Oak King and the Holly King? Didn't you promise the Oak King you would face your fear of death head-on?*

She ignored the voice in her head, concentrating on her work. She stripped the bed without looking at it, tugging the sheets off and replacing them with fresh ones. She blocked out the scent of the room and forced herself not to look at any of the personal items sitting on the bureau or the little table next to the bed. When she left the room, she remembered so little about it that, if asked, she wouldn't have been able to confidently answer a question about what color the walls were.

She went down one entire side of the hallway that way, not looking around the rooms, doing only what was necessary. *It's only your first day*, she reminded herself again and again. *You don't have to do everything all at once*.

When she reached the end of the hall she turned and made her way back up the other side, the wheels of the hamper squeaking as she pushed it. By now she knew exactly what to do, and she was able to get in and out of the rooms quickly. She was anxious to have this part of her day over with as soon as possible. She didn't like being in the empty rooms, surrounded by the scattered belongings of their inhabitants. *I need time to work up to it*, she reassured herself.

At least she was becoming used to the smell. She hardly noticed it now that she had surrounded herself with it. She wondered if the people who lived there ever noticed it, or if it just smelled like home to them. She thought about her own home, and how good it felt to come in the door and smell food cooking in the kitchen or catch the scent of a fire crackling in the big fireplace. She closed her eyes and recalled the smell of the freshly washed sheets on her bed when she snuggled into them at night, and the way the summer breeze carried the perfume of the garden into her window.

What did the people who lived in Shady Hills think of when they thought about the smells of home? she wondered. Did they think of the anti-septic smell of floor cleaners and the harsh bleach that was used to clean their sheets? Annie hoped they had more pleasant associations with the place they lived in, but if they did she had no idea what they were. To her the whole place smelled like it needed someone to open all the windows and let the fresh air in.

She was thinking about this as she entered the last room on the floor. Unlike the other rooms, this one was totally dark because the blinds were completely closed. No light at all came in, and Annie had to turn on the harsh electric light so that she could see what she was doing.

When the light came on she saw that the room was painted a dreary shade of blue. The color had faded to a washed-out gray, and there was no hint of color anywhere to make the place more appealing. The bedspread was the same dull shade, almost like cloudy water, and there weren't any curtains at all on the windows. *This room is about as appealing as a jail cell*, Annie thought as she moved to the bed and began to pull off the sheets.

Trying to hurry, she made the bed in record time, smoothing out the sheets and tucking everything in. She replaced the worn bedspread and gathered up the old sheets in preparation for leaving. She was anxious to get the dirty linen to the laundry room, find Mrs. Abercrombie, and see what was next for her to do. Cleaning rooms that didn't have people in them was starting to feel like tidying up a graveyard.

As she moved to switch off the light, she happened to notice that there was a picture in a frame standing on the battered dresser. Normally the picture wouldn't have drawn her attention, but it was the only thing breaking the otherwise clean surface of the dresser's top, and she thought it was odd that there was nothing else there—no bottles of pills, no comb or brush, nothing to indicate that anyone actually lived in the room.

Annie found herself picking up the picture to look at it. It was an old one, printed in black and white, and the surface of it was creased and wrinkled, as if it had been carried for many years in someone's pocket. It showed two men standing next to each other with their arms around one another's shoulders. They were both dressed in some kind of military uniforms, and they were smiling. *They look a lot alike*, Annie thought as she peered more closely at the image.

As she was looking at the photo the frame suddenly came apart. The back slipped off and fell to the floor, and Annie was left holding the glass and the photograph in her hand. *Great*, she thought, *now I've broken the only thing this person owns*.

She laid the picture carefully on the dresser, glass side down, and bent to retrieve the fallen back. As she did, she noticed that something was written on the back of the photograph. She paused and picked it up again, trying to make out the small, cramped handwriting.

"To Ben," it said. "A guy couldn't ask for a better brother or a better friend. Sorry about the fender. All the best, Tad."

Sorry about the fender? Annie repeated to herself as she put the photo down again, puzzled. What was that supposed to mean? It seemed like a weird thing to write on a photo for someone. Apparently, the men in the picture were brothers. Was one of them the person who lived in the room now?

She reached down and picked up the piece of the frame that was still on the floor. When she stood up again she let out a little shriek—there was a face reflected in the mirror attached to the wall behind the dresser. It was a man's face, and it was angry.

Annie turned and saw an elderly man standing in the doorway, watching her. He was dressed in a blue cardigan and brown pants, and his gray hair was parted neatly on one side and slicked back. One hand rested on the handle of a silver cane, and the other was raised, one finger pointing at Annie.

"What did you do?" the man asked, his voice shaking.

Annie looked at the pieces of the picture frame in her hands. "Oh," she said. "I picked this up and the back accidentally fell off."

"You broke it!" the man said, stepping forward into the room. "You were touching my things and you broke it."

"No," said Annie. "I mean, yes, I touched it. But it isn't broken. See, the back just slides on."

She started to put the frame back together, but

the old man started waving his hand at her. "Just go," he said. "Go on, get out of here. Don't touch that."

He limped over to where Annie stood and made a feeble attempt at grabbing the picture from her. When he did, he knocked both pieces out of her hand. The glass landed on the floor and shattered, sending tiny pieces scattering over the tile. The old man let out a wail.

"It's okay," Annie said, starting to kneel and clean up the mess. "The picture isn't damaged."

"Get out!" the man yelled, shaking his cane. "Leave me alone!"

Annie had never heard someone sound so angry. The old man's voice shook with rage, and she could see his whole body trembling. She wanted to help him, to make things right, but she knew he just wanted her out of his room. Standing up, she tried once more to apologize. "I'm really sorry—" she began.

"Go!" he bellowed. "And don't come back here again."

She opened her mouth to speak, thought better of it, and ran out of the room, leaving the angry old man staring down at the pieces of broken glass. She didn't know what to do. Should she call a janitor or someone to help him clean up the glass? Should she just leave him alone? She wasn't sure. He'd been so angry at her that part of her didn't want to help him at all. *But he looked so sad*, she thought as she hurriedly pushed the laundry cart down the hall away from his room.

She turned the corner and almost ran right over Mrs. Abercrombie, who was walking in the other direction, a clipboard in her hand.

"Whoa there," the nurse said. "Are you in that big of a hurry to get to the next job?"

"I'm sorry," Annie said. "I just had sort of a run-in with one of the patients. I mean, guests," she added, remembering that she'd been instructed never to refer to the residents of Shady Hills in any way that made it sound like they were in a hospital.

"Run-in?" Mrs. Abercrombie said. "What happened?"

Annie explained what had occurred in the room down the hall. When she was finished, she was surprised to hear Mrs. Abercrombie laugh. "That was old Ben Rowe," she said. "Don't mind him. He's the terror of Shady Hills."

"I thought you'd be angry," Annie said. "He sure was."

"Well, you shouldn't have touched anything that belongs to a guest," said the nurse. "But you didn't mean any harm. I'll send someone to help Ben clean up the glass."

"I should probably go apologize," Annie commented.

Mrs. Abercrombie shook her head. "It won't do any good," she said. "Ben hates everyone. We all gave up a long time ago trying to make friends with him. Now we just stay out of his way. Just forget about him. Come on, I'll introduce you to the joys of feeding Jell-O to people with no teeth."

Annie walked away with Mrs. Abercrombie, relieved to be getting as far away as she could from old Ben. *That must have been him in the photo*, she thought as they walked. *Him and his brother.* He'd been so handsome in the picture. She wondered what had happened to make him so miserable and unpleasant. It was hard to imagine the old man who had shaken his cane at her and told her to get out of his room ever being a young, smiling man.

I hope I'm not like that when I'm old, she thought suddenly. *Then again, I hope I'm never in a place like Shady Hills.* But that was something she didn't want to think about. Right now there was Jell-O to deal with.

But you'll have to change Ben's sheets again at some point, she reminded herself with a shudder. She just hoped he wasn't in the room when that time came.

CHAPTER 3

"As you can see from the height of the doorways in this room, people were much shorter in the eighteen hundreds," said Cooper, indicating the door leading from the living room to the little room that used to be Frederick Welton's study.

This was her favorite joke, and she always paused after saying it to see if her audience really believed her or not. To her great delight, this group seemed to be buying it hook, line, and sinker. A few of them were even nodding their heads in agreement, as if she had just confirmed something they'd been telling their friends for years. She suppressed a smile as she turned and led them into the kitchen, saying, "And in here you'll see one of the first coffeemakers in the Pacific Northwest."

It was her second tour of the day. The first had consisted primarily of history buffs who had come to see the former home of Beecher Falls's founding father. That had been a dry affair, as she hadn't been able to fool them with her usual made-up spiel.

She'd just pointed out the various features of the house and then stood back while they snapped pictures. But this second group didn't have the slightest idea what they were looking at. They were there simply because the house was included in a list of things people had to see when they came through town. She'd told them all sorts of ridiculous things, and they'd eaten them up. Luckily, none of it was too off the mark, and she always remembered to throw in the real information so they weren't being cheated out of anything.

At least this beats working at Burger King for six bucks an hour, she told herself as she herded the tourists into the front hallway and up the stairs to the second floor. Sometimes she hated the fact that her family lived in a historic home and was obligated to show people around it, but since she was getting paid for basically giving tours of her bedroom, she didn't complain too much.

"Where does the ghost appear?" a man asked as they ascended the stairs.

"Excuse me?" Cooper said, pretending not to understand.

"The ghost," the man repeated. "Of Frederick Welton. I read somewhere that his ghost still haunts this place."

Cooper laughed. "If he does, I've never seen him," she said.

This was the first outright lie she'd told all day. The truth was that the ghost of Frederick Welton did indeed wander the rooms of his old house, and she *had* seen it. She'd been very little, and she didn't really remember it, but for a while she'd told her mother that a strange man came to visit her every night in her room—the room where Welton had hanged himself after losing his land in a poker game.

But Cooper didn't want to think about ghosts. In fact, she was doing everything she could *not* to think about them. That was all in her past. She didn't see ghosts anymore, and she certainly didn't talk to them. She was through with all of that, through with Wicca and the activities that had led her to see ghosts in the first place.

"But I'm sure I read about a ghost appearing here," the man said stubbornly.

"If you'll look at this painting, you'll see a wonderful example of American folk art," Cooper said quickly, pointing at a picture hanging on the wall of the landing. Even though the picture was one she herself had done in third grade, she hoped it would distract the man and he would stop talking about the ghost. But he was determined.

"In there," he said, pointing to her room. "That's where he did it, isn't it? That's where he killed himself."

Now all of the other members of the group were ignoring the painting and looking with great interest at the door to Cooper's room, which was shut.

"I'm afraid that's part of the private quarters," Cooper said. "We can't go in there."

There were sighs of disappointment from a few people. Cooper knew the man who seemed obsessed with Welton's ghost was going to say something else, so she added quickly, "If you'll follow me to the end of the hall, you can see the room where the infamous poker game took place."

This seemed to distract them, and she ushered the group along the corridor before anyone could say another word about the ghost. *There's always one in every bunch*, she thought. Why couldn't they just forget about the whole haunted house thing?

But the man wasn't through yet. As he walked past Cooper he looked at her curiously. He paused, continued walking, and then stopped and turned around.

"I knew I recognized you," he said. "You're Cooper Rivers, right?"

Cooper didn't know what to say. She sensed something unpleasant was about to happen, but she couldn't very well deny being who she was. After all, her family's name was on the mailbox on the front porch.

"That's right," she said. "Now, if you'll all follow—"

"You're the one who talked to the dead girl," the man continued. "What was her name? Elizabeth something."

Now everyone in the group was staring openly

at Cooper. They'd forgotten all about the poker game and Frederick Welton. Cooper glared at the man who had started all the trouble, wishing she could push him down the stairs.

Elizabeth Sanger, she thought to herself. *You mean Elizabeth Sanger.* But she didn't say anything out loud. If the man wanted to talk about what had happened, he would have to do it on his own. Cooper wasn't about to give him any help.

"Sanger," he said, as if reading her mind. "It was Elizabeth Sanger. She was murdered, and you said her ghost talked to you. I read it in the paper."

"They exaggerated a little," Cooper said curtly. "Now, if we can continue with the tour—"

"Did you really talk to her ghost?" the man asked, interrupting again.

"It wasn't exactly like that," Cooper said. "But that doesn't have anything to do with Welton House, so let's stick with the tour."

"I can't believe you don't want to talk about it," the man continued stubbornly. "If I saw a ghost, let alone talked to one, I'd be telling everyone about it."

"Then let's hope you never see one," Cooper said, her temper getting the better of her.

She charged past the man and continued down the hallway, hoping the group would follow her. The man was really pushing her buttons. Why couldn't people let her forget about what had happened with the ghost of Elizabeth Sanger? It seemed the harder she tried to get away from those events the more they loomed over her. *Mom was right*, she thought angrily. *Getting involved with witchcraft just causes problems.*

But then you would never have met Kate and Annie, she reminded herself. That was certainly true. But more and more she was having a hard time figuring out how to fit her friends into her life now that she'd given up her Wiccan studies. She was the one who had decided to stop studying the Craft. She was the one who'd had the horrible experience at the Midsummer Eve ritual in the woods back in June. She had made her choice, and she didn't expect them to do it, too, or even to agree with it. She knew that following the Wiccan path had to be a personal decision that each person made independently. But she hadn't even called them since they'd gotten back. She didn't know what to say to them, and although she kept thinking she would find a way to explain to them how she felt, more and more time went by without their speaking. Now she was afraid that time might have run out. When she stopped at the room at the end of the hall and turned around, she was thankful to see that the group had indeed followed her. They were looking at her oddly, and she knew they were dying to ask her more about seeing ghosts. But she didn't give them the chance.

"This is where Frederick Welton and Seymour Beecher played the card game that lost Welton the land that became Beecher Falls," she said, beginning the rehearsed speech she'd given a hundred times before. She continued talking, not deviating from the official script, and when she was done she smiled brightly. "And that concludes our tour. Thank you for coming. If you go back the way you came you can exit through the front door."

She walked quickly past the group, pointedly avoiding looking at the man who had asked so many questions, and went down the stairs. Opening the front door, she nodded politely to the guests as they left the house. When the last one was gone, she went back inside, climbed the stairs to her room, and threw herself down on the bed with a sigh. Looking up, she stared at the beam over her bed. It was from that very beam that Frederick Welton had hanged himself nearly a hundred and fifty years before. She'd slept underneath it since she was a little girl, and she'd always been fascinated by the story of Welton's death. But now she wanted to forget all about him and his ghost. About *all* ghosts.

She sat up and looked at the table where, until she'd dismantled it, her altar had been. Now the things that had once covered the altar were in a box in her closet—the picture of Elizabeth Sanger, the statue of the goddess Pele that Kate had given her, and the scrying bowl that had been a gift from Annie. She hadn't thrown anything away. The presents from her friends meant a lot to her, even if she wasn't going to use them, and she still liked to remember Elizabeth and how she'd helped solve the mystery of Elizabeth's death. She just didn't want to talk about it. And she definitely didn't want to do it ever again.

It was difficult for her to realize that less than two weeks before she had been excited about going up into the woods with her friends to celebrate the sabbat of Litha. That seemed like such a long time ago. But that one night in the forest had changed everything. She'd been chased around by a bunch of insane kids calling themselves faeries, made to act the part of a hunted animal in some bizarre ritual they'd concocted to tease her. It had been a horrible experience, one made even worse by the fact that Annie and Kate had both had incredibly life-changing nights and that when Cooper had told the organizers of the event about what had happened to her they'd told her that none of them knew any kids like the ones she described meeting. Even though she gave them all the names she could remember, and described in detail what the so-called faeries had looked like and what had happened, they kept telling her that they didn't know anyone who fit her descriptions.

Frustrated, she'd decided to give up on Wicca. If getting involved with rituals and the people who participated in them could land her in that kind of trouble, she didn't want any further part of it. She'd been really upset by what had happened to her, and it bothered her that no one could give her an explanation for the events or help her find the people who had done those things to her.

What she hadn't told anyone—not even Kate and Annie—was that she wasn't entirely sure what had really happened that night. It had all seemed so real at the time, and she could still recall the faces of Bird, Spider, and the other kids she'd been chased by. She remembered sitting in the Cave of Visions and being surrounded by weird purple smoke, and she recalled jumping from a high place into a pool of cold water. She even remembered snatches of the beautiful music Bird had been playing on her flute, the music that had lured Cooper into the woods in the first place.

But somewhere, somehow, things had changed. She'd lost control of what was happening to her, and that was the part that really frightened her. At some point she had been swept up in whatever magic was running wild in the woods that night. She had felt hunted by the very thing she'd been seeking out through her own magical work. The kids pretending to be faeries had laughed at her, chased her, and made her feel like a fool. In the end she'd escaped them, but in the process everything she'd ever thought she knew about Wicca and magic had been turned upside down. That's why she needed to get away from it.

Her parents, if they noticed that she'd taken down her altar, hadn't said anything. And she certainly wasn't going to bring it up, especially after all of the trouble her involvement in Wicca had caused in the first place. It had taken enormous amounts of effort to convince her mother that going to the weekly study class was a good idea, particularly after her brush with Elizabeth Sanger's ghost had resulted first in her name's appearing in the local paper and then in Annie's being kidnapped by the girl's murderer. Mrs. Rivers had her own doubts about witchcraft stemming from a long-ago argument with her mother over teaching Cooper spells when she was a child, and seeing her daughter involved in the same thing had been a lot for her to deal with. Cooper didn't want to admit that perhaps her mother had been right about the dangers of practicing magic, even if she herself had similar doubts.

Instead, she had poured herself into her music. Now that she was spending less time reading about the Craft and experimenting with the different aspects of it, she had more time for her songs. She'd been writing a lot, and had come up with a bunch of new lyrics and music that she was anxious to experiment with. There were a couple of open-mike events coming up at local coffeehouses, and she was thinking about maybe trying out some of her stuff there in the next couple of months.

She picked up her guitar and started fooling around with a melody line she'd come up with the night before. It felt good to just play, to let herself get lost in the music. The notes seemed to fall into place easily, and soon she had turned the short phrase into a longer one. She played it again and again, trying it out and changing a note here and there until she had something she really liked. She played it again.

Something about that sounds really familiar, she thought suddenly. But what was it? She played the music again, listening carefully. Was it something she'd heard on the radio? She didn't think so, as she usually always remembered other people's songs. But there was definitely something about the music that she had heard before.

Then it hit her—she was playing part of the faerie music. It was a snippet of the song that Spider and the others had played as part of her "test" to see if she was good enough to join them. She had re-created it almost exactly as she'd heard it. Although she'd done her best to push that night from her mind, here it was coming back to her, and through the one thing she thought was hers and hers alone— her music.

Angrily, she put down the guitar and stared at her hands. Why couldn't she get away from the memories of that night? Why did she have to keep thinking about it? The song had seemed so beautiful to her before she remembered its true source. It hadn't come from her own imagination; it had come from Spider's, and from the instruments of the awful kids who had put her through such a terrifying ordeal.

Great, she thought, *now you're in my music, too.*

She sighed. This wasn't like her. Normally nothing could get to her. She'd always prided herself on being tough, invincible. She liked it that the other kids at school were sort of afraid of her. She'd even liked it in the beginning when Kate had been afraid of her, and the reason she'd taken to Annie so quickly was because she'd been strong enough to stand up to her. Very few people could do that. Just as very few people could make her doubt herself. But that's what Spider and the others had done. Even Bird, who had helped her out in the end, had left her with more questions than answers. Nothing about that night made sense, and now she was being reminded of it all over again.

Just then the phone rang, interrupting her thoughts. She was glad to have a distraction, though, and she picked it up with a relieved "Hello?"

"Hey," said a guy's voice. "It's me."

Cooper relaxed. It was T.J. He was probably the one person she really didn't mind hearing from right then. In fact, lately she'd started looking forward to hearing from him.

"What's up?" she asked, trying to sound casual.

"Not much," he said. "I just happened to score two tickets for the Blink-182 show Thursday night at the Forum, and I thought I'd see if you wanted to go."

Do I want to go? Cooper thought. *Of course I want to go!*

"I guess," she said.

"Cool," said T.J. "I'll come by around seven,

unless you want to get together earlier and get something to eat. Or whatever. We don't have to if you'd rather not."

"Hey, a girl has to eat," Cooper replied. "How about we meet at the pizza place by the club at six?"

"Sure," T.J. answered. "See you then."

Cooper hung up. She was surprised at how much she was looking forward to the evening. But was it because she was seeing Blink-182 or because she was seeing them with T.J.? She'd been to a lot of shows. In fact, she'd seen Blink-182 about six months before at a concert in Seattle. But the idea of seeing them now—with T.J.—made her smile.

Oh, come on, she told herself. *Don't tell me you're turning into one of those dopey spritz-heads who gets all weird whenever a boy calls. It's just T.J.*

She got up and looked in the mirror. "Maybe those faeries did more to you than just chase you through the woods," she said out loud. "Because you are definitely *not* acting like yourself."

It was true; she wasn't acting like the old Cooper. Something about her was different. It was like everything had been turned upside down and she was suddenly seeing the world in a different way. But she would have to wait until later to sort it all out. Right now she had to decide what she was going to wear when she met T.J.

CHAPTER 4

Kate looked at her aunt through the viewfinder of the camera, trying to center her exactly. Aunt Netty was standing on the end of the pier, leaning against one of the posts. She was wearing a bright red shirt, and Kate liked how the color contrasted with the clear blue sky and the darker green of the ocean.

"I think you could paint me faster than you're taking that picture," Aunt Netty joked.

"Just a second," Kate said. "I want it to be perfect." She focused the lens and pressed her finger down on the button. The camera whirred to life, and Kate lowered it. "Okay," she said. "I think that shot will definitely make the cover of the *Sports Illustrated* swimsuit issue."

"I'm glad I went for the thong bikini then," said her aunt.

Kate was having another great day. She and her aunt had spent the morning shopping, trying on clothes and behaving like a couple of best friends. That was one of the things Kate liked best about

Aunt Netty—she didn't treat Kate like a kid, the way her parents sometimes did. She treated her like an equal, asking her opinions about things and seeking her advice on what she should wear or what colors of makeup would look best on her. They'd had a wonderful time, and each of them had emerged from the stores with several new items.

Now they were taking pictures. As always, Aunt Netty had brought her camera with her. For as long as Kate could remember, she'd been asking her aunt to teach her how to take good photographs. But Aunt Netty had always been too busy, or there were other things to do instead. Now, though, she was showing her niece how to use the camera she herself used on many of her assignments.

"You want to look for interesting juxtapositions," her aunt said as she came over and stood behind Kate. "Look over there, for instance. See how that cloud swoops down and looks like it's touching the ocean?"

Kate looked in the direction in which her aunt was pointing. Sure enough, she saw the cloud Aunt Netty was talking about. It really did look like a hand reaching out of the sky to stroke the surface of the sea. She raised the camera and was going to snap a photo when she felt her aunt tapping her on the shoulder. She turned and saw her pointing silently at something behind them.

Kate's eyes followed her aunt's gaze, and she saw what had caught her attention. A little girl was standing at the side of the wharf, holding an ice-cream cone. But she wasn't paying attention, and the cone was tilting toward the nose of an interested black Labrador retriever who was sitting beside her. The dog was sniffing the air, and his tongue was perilously close to the girl's treat.

Kate quickly lifted the camera. She focused in on the little girl and the dog just as the Lab, unable to wait any longer, reached over and took a big lick of the cone. The little girl turned and shrieked happily just as Kate clicked the shutter. She took several more shots as the dog quickly consumed the ice cream, and the girl's mother and the dog's father both watched, startled, before breaking into loud laughter.

"Those are the kinds of moments you can't plan," Aunt Netty said as Kate handed her back the camera. "But now you've caught it forever, and every time you look at those pictures you'll remember how that little girl looked and how happy the dog was."

Kate looked at her aunt's face as she spoke. There was a look in her eyes that Kate couldn't really read. It was as if she was thinking about the thing she loved most in the world, but instead of being totally happy about it she was kind of sad, too. Kate almost asked her what she was thinking, but something told her it was a moment her aunt wanted to keep for herself.

"Why don't we go get some lunch?" Aunt Netty

said, breaking the silence. "I don't know about you, but I'm starving."

They walked to the end of the pier to a restaurant that had a big deck with tables that overlooked the water. The waiter led them to one that was partially shaded by a big umbrella, and they sat down. As Kate perused the menu, she felt the sun on her skin and smelled the sea breeze and decided that it was going to be the best summer ever.

"Any idea what you want?" asked her aunt.

"The clam strips sound great," Kate answered. "But I think that's an awful lot of fat. Maybe I should just have the grilled chicken salad."

"Go for the clam strips," replied her aunt. "Life's too short to worry about a little bit of fat. In fact, I insist that you have the clam strips *and* the cheesecake afterward."

"Well, if you *insist*," Kate said, closing her menu.

The waiter appeared, and Kate gave him her order. When it was Aunt Netty's turn she ordered grilled red snapper.

"Oh, so I'm supposed to order the fattening stuff while you eat healthy, is that it?" Kate said when the waiter had taken their menus.

Her aunt put her arms on the table and leaned forward. "When you're thirty-four years old and can't fit into your favorite jeans anymore, *then* you can worry about what you eat," she said. "Until then, enjoy yourself."

Kate giggled. "But you look great," she said. "I

don't think I've ever seen you so thin before."

For a moment it looked as if Aunt Netty's smile faltered. But then she perked up again. "So tell me about your life," she said. "And I don't mean what you want to do this summer or anything like that. Tell me all the stuff you don't tell your mother."

Kate leaned back in her chair and took a sip of iced tea. What should she tell her aunt? It was true that they were more like best friends than relatives. She had always told Aunt Netty everything, even the things she was afraid to share with her parents. She never worried that her aunt would tell anyone else, and she'd always believed that she could tell her anything.

But was that true? Could she, for instance, tell Aunt Netty that she had been studying Wicca for almost four months, and that she'd gotten into it because she'd done a spell that landed her the boyfriend she'd so recently dumped? Could she tell her aunt that she had a makeshift altar in her bedroom, and that sometimes when no one else was home she did rituals to the Goddess? What would Aunt Netty think of her then? Would Kate still be her favorite niece, or would everything change? Kate didn't know, and for the first time in her life she'd found something she couldn't tell her aunt about.

"Well, you know about Tyler," Kate said, trying to buy time. "Things are going really well with him. And Annie and Cooper are okay, too. I hate to sound boring, but everything is pretty much fine. I don't throw up my dinner. I'm not using any controlled substances. And I haven't sent anyone naked pictures of myself over the Internet in a couple of months now."

"Very funny," Aunt Netty said. "But there must be *something* going on in the life of Katherine Elaine Morgan."

Kate rolled her eyes. She hated her full name, and her aunt knew it. She only used it when she wanted to tease Kate. Now Kate wished more than anything that she could tell Aunt Netty about her involvement in witchcraft. But she just couldn't. She wasn't ready to take that risk. Not yet.

"I'm serious," she said. "There's nothing going on. I'm going to be the most boring junior at Beecher Falls High School. But what about you? What's this assignment you're here on? Something good, I hope."

Her aunt took a long drink and looked out over the water for a minute. When she turned back to Kate she sighed and said, "There's something your mother and I have been keeping from you," she said. "She didn't want me to tell you, but I think it's time you knew."

"Don't tell me you're getting married," Kate said excitedly, remembering how her mother had seemed so nervous about Kate's asking personal questions the night before and putting two and two together.

Her aunt laughed. "No," she said. "I'm not getting married. At least not any time soon. You kind of need a man for that anyway."

"I don't get it, then," Kate said. "What's the big secret?"

"There's something I want to show you," said her aunt. "Remember how you said my hair was shorter than last time you saw me?"

Kate nodded. Then she watched as Aunt Netty reached up, removed her hat, and lifted her hair clear off of her head. The hair dangled from her hand as she waved it around, and Kate stared in shock at her head.

"You're bald!" she said.

"Surprise," said her aunt, putting her straw hat back on. "Do you like it? I hear it's all the rage now."

"You're bald!" Kate said again, not believing what she was seeing.

Her aunt plopped the wig onto the table, where Kate stared at it as if it might leap up and bite her. "That's the big secret?" she asked. "You've been wearing a wig?"

Her aunt laughed. "Actually, the wig is a relatively new development," she said.

Kate was confused. "I don't get it," she said.

Aunt Netty reached out and took Kate's hand. "I'd like to tell you that I'm making some grand statement about fashion, or even that I've become a Buddhist," she said. "But, honey, the truth is that I'm not here on any assignment. I have cancer."

Kate shook her head. "What did you say?" she asked.

"Cancer," said her aunt. "I have cancer. That's why I'm wearing a wig. My hair fell out after the last round of chemo. I know finding out like this must be more than a little strange for you, but I didn't really know how else to do it. I figured just jumping in would get the shock over with as quickly as possible."

Kate was stunned. She didn't know what to say. Was her aunt kidding? It would be just like her to shave her head. But pretending she had cancer? She would never joke about something like that.

"When?" was all Kate could say. "How? Why?"

"I found out about three months ago," her aunt explained. "I discovered a lump in my breast while I was showering. I went to the doctor, he did a biopsy, and voilà—I had cancer."

Kate looked into her aunt's face. There were the familiar brown eyes, the nose that looked just like her mother's nose and her own nose, the mouth that was smiling the reassuring smile that had comforted Kate many times. But with her hair gone, Aunt Netty looked different. She was changed. And that change was because of the cancer inside of her.

"I know I should have told you earlier," Aunt Netty said. "You and I have never had secrets from each other, and I didn't want to start now. But I wanted to do it in person, and I thought I would wait until the lump was gone and I was okay again."

Kate felt herself beginning to cry. Partly she was devastated by the news of her aunt's illness. But more than that, she felt even more terrible about not being able to talk to Aunt Netty about Wicca. Here she was, battling cancer, and Kate couldn't even talk to her about something as simple as her own spirituality.

"Don't start that," Aunt Netty said, handing Kate a napkin. "If you cry then I'll cry, and then this will all be way too much like a bad after-school special."

Kate laughed despite herself. She dabbed at her eyes with the napkin, then looked down at the wig sitting beside her aunt's bread plate. "Are you going to put that back on?" she asked.

"I don't think so," her aunt replied. "I sort of dropped it in the butter. Besides, I never liked it. Now that I don't have to pretend anymore, I think I'll stick with the hat look."

Aunt Netty took the wig and put it in the bag she'd been carrying with her. Then she took out a bottle of pills, opened it, and popped one in her mouth.

"So it wasn't just a headache," Kate said, suddenly remembering the incident from the night before. "And that's why you didn't eat much yesterday, and why Dad kept telling you to take it easy."

Her aunt nodded. "I'm really sorry I didn't tell you earlier," she said. "I'd hoped this would turn out to be nothing and that I could tell everyone when it was all over."

"But it isn't over?" asked Kate fearfully.

Her aunt shook her head. "The lump was larger than we thought, and it turned out that the cancer had spread to some of my lymph nodes," she answered. "That's when I had the chemo and my hair fell out. Unfortunately, that still didn't get it all. That's why I'm here. The hospital here has a terrific cancer treatment center. My doctor has basically done everything he can. We want to see if this is any better."

Kate looked down at her hands, which were twisting her napkin into a ball. There was a question she desperately wanted to ask, but she was almost equally afraid of the answer she might get.

At that moment the waiter arrived, bringing them their lunches. As he set the plates in front of them he glanced briefly at Aunt Netty's bare head under her hat before looking away. Kate noticed his reaction and wanted to say "She has cancer." She knew the waiter was wondering, and she didn't like the idea of people looking at her aunt and thinking there was something wrong with her. But the waiter just asked them if they would like anything else, and when they shook their heads he walked away as if they were having a perfectly normal lunch.

Only it wasn't a perfectly normal lunch. It might have been when they'd sat down, but everything had changed as soon as Aunt Netty had uttered those three words that Kate was sure she would never get out of her head: "I have cancer."

"Are you going to die?" she asked suddenly, the question she'd been unable to voice tumbling out of her mouth before she could stop it.

Her aunt paused, a forkful of red snapper halfway to her mouth, and looked into Kate's eyes. "I don't know," she said. "I know that's not the answer you want. It's not the answer I want either. But it's the truth. I'm not sure what will happen next."

"You're right," Kate said. "That's not what I wanted to hear."

She looked at the pile of clam strips in front of her. Just the thought of eating one made her feel sick to her stomach. The idea of ever eating anything again seemed impossible. How could she enjoy food when her favorite aunt was dying? What she wanted to do was scream and cry and tell everyone how unfair it was that someone so smart and funny and beautiful could be filled with something that was eating her up from the inside.

"It won't do any good," her aunt said, interrupting her thoughts.

"What won't do any good?" Kate asked.

"Not eating," said Aunt Netty. "I tried that. I tried crying a lot and trying to figure out what caused it, too, but that didn't work either. Trust me—I've tried pretty much everything, and it doesn't do any good. But you know what *does* help?"

"What?" asked Kate glumly when her aunt paused.

"Cheesecake," said Aunt Netty. "There isn't a problem in the world that cheesecake can't solve. Why do you think I had you order it?"

She gave Kate a huge smile, and Kate couldn't help but give her a little one back. She still felt a great big knot of pain and fear in her stomach, but seeing her aunt smile made it loosen a little bit. *Maybe even enough to fit a clam strip in there*, she thought, picking up one of the fried pieces and dipping it in the bowl of tartar sauce on the side of her plate.

"That's my girl," said Aunt Netty. "So, do you have any other questions, besides the one about my imminent demise?"

"I don't know," Kate said. "I've never known anyone who had—" She paused, not knowing how to finish. "Who had what you have," she said finally.

"Cancer," said her aunt. "I have cancer. I know it's an ugly word, but you make it uglier when you don't say it."

"Cancer," Kate said, hating the sound of it. "I've never known anyone who had cancer."

"I'll give you the crash course, then," her aunt said. "Basically, I have these cells in my body that, for one reason or another, are behaving abnormally. They divide and form new cells when they aren't supposed to, and this forms tumors. Eventually, these cells can begin to destroy surrounding organs."

"They can't just take the tumors out?" Kate asked.

Aunt Netty nodded. "That's what we did first,"

she said. "But the cancer had already spread to other parts of my body. Now we're trying to stop it from spreading any more."

"How?" Kate asked.

"Various things," her aunt explained. "I'll be happy to explain all of it later. But right now let's just have lunch. We have my whole visit to talk about medical things."

"When do you go into the hospital?" asked Kate.

"Tomorrow," her aunt informed her. "This may be my last chance to have cheesecake for a while, so let's enjoy it. Maybe I'll even get *two* pieces. I'm feeling pretty good today."

So was I, Kate thought as she picked up another clam strip and put it into her mouth. *At least until a few minutes ago.*

CHAPTER 5

Annie walked into Shady Hills on Thursday morning wishing she was anyplace else. Her run-in with Ben Rowe on Tuesday had gotten things off to a bad start. Although she hadn't seen the old man at all on her second day, the memory of his anger was still fresh in her mind. To make everything even worse, Kate had called her the night before, distraught, to tell her that her aunt had cancer. Annie had never heard her friend so upset before, and while she had tried to comfort Kate as much as she could, she knew she wasn't very good at that kind of thing. In fact, hearing Kate's news had brought back a lot of memories that Annie hadn't wanted to face, at least not quite yet.

As much as she'd been tempted to call in sick, or even to quit altogether, Annie had made a promise to Mrs. Abercrombie—and to herself. So she pushed open the doors of the nursing home and went inside. As she walked toward the nursing office she thought about what they had discussed in their Wicca study group on Tuesday night. Because it was summer, a number of people were on vacation or away until Jasper College started up again in September, so the study group was smaller than usual. Instead of their usual format, they were meeting more informally to talk about what was happening in their lives and to discuss any particular issues they were having with their individual progress.

Annie had been particularly anxious for Tuesday's meeting because of what had happened at work that day. Being with other people who were studying witchcraft relaxed her and made her feel like she was part of an extended family. She knew she could talk about what had happened with her friends and maybe they would have some advice for dealing with her feelings.

She'd been right. When she told the group what had happened with Ben Rowe, Sophia had nodded her head knowingly. "Remember at your initiation, when we told you that there would be a lot of challenges as you walked the path for a year and a day?" she'd asked. "Well, sometimes those challenges come in the form of people. It sounds like you've tripped right over one."

Now, passing by the rooms of the people who lived at Shady Hills, Annie thought more about that idea. She'd decided to volunteer at the nursing home for the summer because she thought it would help her face something in her life that she'd been struggling with for many years. She'd had the idea after the Midsummer ritual she and her friends had attended, at which she'd come face-to-face with her fear of death, and particularly with her unresolved sadness over the deaths of her parents when she was a little girl. Coming into a place where people were living out the ends of their lives seemed like a good way for her to start accepting that part of the cycle of nature, and she'd been proud of herself for taking that step.

But now she appeared to be facing a new hurdle, on only her third day. She'd been hoping to ease into things gradually. But if Sophia was right, she had instead fallen headlong into things from the very first minute thanks to Ben Rowe and his stupid picture. While she felt badly about breaking the frame, Annie couldn't help resenting the old man a little bit. She had only been trying to help. He was the one who had knocked the glass from her hands. He was the one who had screamed at her for no reason. Why should *she* feel sorry about anything? *Ben Rowe isn't a challenge*, she thought grimly. *He's just a nasty old man.* And if she had anything to say about it, she was going to stay as far away from him as she possibly could.

"Look who's back," Mrs. Abercrombie said when Annie entered the nurses' room. She was sitting at her desk, looking at something on her ever-present clipboard, and she seemed to be in a good mood.

"Hi," said Annie. "What's on the schedule for

today? Do you want me to start doing the beds?"

Mrs. Abercrombie shook her head. "Not today, sweetie," she said brightly. "Today we have an event."

"An event?" Annie repeated, not understanding.

"Every so often we have someone come in to do some kind of program for the guests," the nurse explained. "You know, school choirs that come in and sing at Christmas. People who come by and lead Bingo Night. That kind of thing."

Annie nodded. "I get it," she said. "So what's today's event?"

"How do you feel about magic?" asked Mrs. Abercrombie.

"Magic?" Annie said, wondering what the woman was getting at. "What do you mean?" Was it possible, she wondered, that Mrs. Abercrombie somehow knew about her involvement with Wicca?

"We have a magician coming in today," explained the nurse. "He needs an assistant."

"Oh, that kind of magic," Annie said.

Mrs. Abercrombie raised one eyebrow. "Is there another kind?" she asked.

Annie reddened. "No," she said. "I guess not. I just didn't know what you meant."

"So how about it?" said the nurse. "Do you feel like being sawed in half or pulling rabbits out of a hat, or whatever it is this guy needs?"

"If it means I don't have to change thirty beds, sure," Annie answered.

"Then come with me," Mrs. Abercrombie said, standing up. "I'll introduce you to the wizard."

Annie followed the nurse out of the office and down the hall toward the recreation room. She had no idea what she was getting herself into, but she figured it couldn't be any worse than changing sheets. *Besides*, she thought, *you might learn a few tricks*.

When they entered the room, Annie saw that a black curtain had been hung up at one end of it. There were several boxes sitting in front of the curtain, and a man was taking things out of them. He was short, with fiery red hair and a little goatee. When he saw Annie and Mrs. Abercrombie he gave them a big smile and waved them over.

"Come in," he said. "I was just starting to set up."

"Annie," Mrs. Abercrombie said as they approached the man, "allow me to introduce the Amazing Rudolpho."

"You can call me Rudy," the man said, shaking Annie's hand. "Rudolpho is just my stage name."

Annie suppressed a smile as she greeted the magician. He was a funny character, like something out of an old-time stage show, and she liked him instantly. Even his name made her laugh to herself.

"I guess I'm your assistant for the day," Annie said.

Rudy grinned and clapped his hands. "And what a beautiful assistant you are!" he said happily. "Tell me, how do you feel about snakes?"

When he saw the look on Annie's face he waved a hand at her. "Just kidding," he said. "But I might ask you to hold a dove or two if that's okay."

"As long as it isn't a reptile I'm okay with it," Annie answered.

"I've got to get back to work," Mrs. Abercrombie said. "I'll be back at eleven when it's showtime."

After the nurse left, Rudy gestured to the boxes he had been unpacking. "Why don't you help me set up," he said to Annie. "I can explain what we'll be doing as we go along."

He turned to a box and pulled out a wand. When he handed it to Annie it suddenly burst to life, and flowers came shooting out the end. Startled, Annie jumped back.

"You have to be prepared for anything this morning," Rudy said, laughing.

He showed Annie how to retract the paper flowers back into the wand, and she placed it on the table that he had already set up. Then he took out some more items, showing her what each one did before putting it in its place on the table. There were rings that seemed to pass through one another, scarves that could be pulled out of a closed fist or even Rudy's mouth, and the standard magician's hat with a false bottom for hiding things in.

"There's nothing too tricky here," Rudy told Annie as she surveyed the props. "I'll just ask you to hand me things when I need them. Otherwise you can just stand there and look mysterious."

"Do you do a lot of these shows?" Annie asked him.

Rudy nodded. "I mostly do birthdays for five-year-olds," he said. "But I like to visit the older folks when I get a chance. As you probably know, it's not exactly a barrel of laughs in a place like this."

"I get that impression," said Annie, arranging a deck of cards and some handcuffs on the table.

"But you and I get to leave at the end of the day," Rudy commented. "They don't."

Annie thought about that as she continued to unpack Rudy's things. He was right. When she left, the unpleasant smells and the air of sadness stayed behind. But what must it be like to live with them every second of every day? No wonder people like Ben Rowe were so unpleasant. *You probably would be, too, if you lived like this,* she thought.

For the next hour Rudy showed Annie the various tricks he would be performing. It was fascinating to see how they worked. Even though most of them had very simple explanations, they still appeared magical when you didn't know how they were done. It made Annie think about real magic, the kind she and the others involved in Wicca sometimes did. That appeared easy, too, to people who didn't really understand it. But the fact was that performing magic correctly took a lot of skill and practice. While at first she'd thought of the Amazing Rudolpho as something of a joke, now she wondered if maybe they didn't have more in common than she'd believed.

A little before eleven people started entering

the room. Many of them walked in on their own, while others were wheeled in or helped along by nurses or friends who could move a little better than they could. They took their seats in the folding chairs that had been set up, and they looked toward the front of the room expectantly.

Annie and Rudy were behind the black curtain, waiting. Rudy had changed into his magician's outfit—a black suit with a cape. He had given Annie something to wear as well, a long black robe that covered her street clothes and made her feel like she was part of a choir or something.

"It's showtime," Rudy said as the last of the old people came in and settled down. "You ready?"

Annie nodded and followed Rudy as he stepped out through the part in the curtains. The audience applauded weakly as Rudy bowed to them and announced in a dramatic voice, "Ladies and gentlemen, welcome to the world of magic."

Annie looked out at the sea of faces. Some of them were clearly interested in what was going on, but others just seemed bewildered by it all. A few were even sleeping, their heads lolling to one side as they dozed in the sunlight that came in the room's windows.

Rudy didn't seem at all discouraged by the lack of enthusiasm from his audience. He launched into his first trick—the floating rings—as if he were performing at the biggest circus on the planet. Annie watched as he moved the rings around, pretending to pull them through each other with great effort. When he handed them to her, she raised them up as the crowd clapped before she put them back on the table.

Rudy worked his way through trick after trick, and Annie dutifully helped whenever he asked for her assistance. Several times Rudy asked the crowd to "give a hand for my lovely assistant," and Annie blushed as she saw the old people take their eyes away from him for a moment to stare at her.

After performing a trick in which he made a card disappear into thin air, Rudy turned to the audience. "And now it's time for some crowd participation," he said. "Can I have a volunteer?"

When no hands went up, Annie saw Rudy scan the crowd for someone to call on. She wondered what kind of trick he was going to do. He hadn't told her about anything that would involve someone else. But everything else had been easy enough for her to do, so she figured this would be easy, too.

"You," Rudy said, pointing at someone. "How about you? You look like you could help me work some magic."

He walked into the sea of chairs, and Annie looked to see where he was heading. Rudy went straight to the back and reached out to someone Annie couldn't see at first because he was behind someone in a wheelchair. Then she watched, horrified, as Rudy walked back up the aisle with a muttering Ben Rowe in tow. The old man seemed to be trying to pull away from the magician, but Rudy wasn't letting him get away.

"Trust me," he said as he led Ben to a spot next to Annie. "My assistant and I will take good care of you."

Ben didn't even give Annie a second glance, but she found her heart racing as she stood beside him. Did he recognize her? Did he remember what had happened in his room on Tuesday? If he did, he gave no indication of it. He just stood there, awkwardly looking at his feet and mumbling something under his breath.

Rudy picked something off the prop table and walked over to Ben. He was holding a piece of newspaper in his hands. He showed it to the crowd and then rolled it into a funnel shape.

"I'm going to ask this handsome gentleman to hold this for me," he said, handing the newspaper to Ben. "And then I'm going to ask my assistant to perform the magic."

Annie looked at Rudy, her eyes wide. *She* was going to perform the trick? But she didn't know anything about magic. Not that kind, at least. What was Rudy thinking?

"Don't worry," he whispered to her as he took her hand and led her to the table. "This one is foolproof. All you have to do is pour the milk into the newspaper funnel. The jug has a fake bottom to it. Just hold down the button underneath the handle and the milk will be sucked into the bottom. Not a drop will actually go into the paper."

He handed Annie the pitcher of milk. It was very heavy, and she held it with both hands as she walked back to where Ben Rowe was standing with the newspaper funnel in his hands.

"Watch as my assistant makes this milk disappear into thin air," Rudy exclaimed as Annie lifted the pitcher to show everyone that it was full. He turned and winked at her, reassuring her that she could do it.

Annie leaned the pitcher toward the opening of the funnel. She watched as the milk flowed toward the lip of the pitcher. She was so nervous about spilling any that she could hardly think. As the milk slipped over the lip of the jug and began to fall into the funnel, she let out a sigh of relief. She hadn't spilled it.

Then, too late, she realized that she'd completely forgotten about the button. She'd been so anxious about spilling the milk, it had slipped her mind. Now she fumbled for the button. But even as her finger found it and pressed, she watched, helpless, as the milk filled up the bottom of the funnel. The paper bulged wetly for a moment. Then it burst, and milk poured all down the front of Ben Rowe and splashed onto his shoes.

Annie pulled the pitcher back as the old man stared at his sopping wet clothes in confusion, the tattered remains of the funnel clutched in his hands. Annie couldn't move. She felt Rudy come and take the pitcher from her, and she only came to her senses when she heard him say, "It looks like my lovely assistant forgot to say the magic word."

Ben Rowe looked up at Annie, his eyes blazing. She knew then that he *did* recognize her, and she wanted to die. Before he could say anything, she turned and ran from the room. She saw some of the old people turn to stare at her as she went, but she couldn't stop.

Once she was in the hallway she leaned against the wall and forced herself not to cry. She could hear Rudy through the doorway, somehow smoothing over the disaster she'd caused. She knew she should go back in and help him finish the show, but she couldn't. She couldn't face everyone, especially not Ben Rowe. It was too much.

Instead, she waited until the show was over. Her trick had apparently been the last one planned, so she only had to wait while Rudy said good-bye to the crowd and they clapped one final time. Then people started coming out again. Annie ducked behind a corner and waited as they filed out. She didn't want them to see her there. She especially didn't want to see Ben Rowe come out with his wet clothes.

When she was sure that the room was empty she went back in. Rudy was putting away the props from his show. Annie sheepishly walked over to him.

"I am *so* sorry," she said. "I know I ruined everything."

Rudy laughed. "Don't worry about it," he said. "Do you know how many times one of these props has frozen up on me? I swear sometimes they have minds of their own."

"It wasn't the pitcher," Annie said. "It was me. I just forgot because I was nervous. That man you picked from the audience and I have kind of a history."

Rudy cocked his head. "He seems a little old for you," he said, feigning seriousness.

Annie laughed in spite of her unhappiness. "Not that kind of history," she said. "I sort of broke something that belonged to him a few days ago. I don't think I'm his favorite person around here. After today I'm sure I'm not."

"He'll forget about it," Rudy said. "Give him a few days."

Annie shook her head. "I don't think this guy forgets anything," she said. "I think he's just mean."

Rudy chuckled. "Or lonely," he said as he took the now-infamous pitcher and put it back in the box.

"What do you mean?" asked Annie.

"I run into a lot of people who seem unfriendly," Rudy said. "Five-year-old kids who refuse to enjoy their own birthday parties. Parents who try to push me around. Old men who act like they don't need anyone. It's easy to write them off. But what I've found is that often what they really want is for someone to keep trying to get in."

"I don't know," Annie said. "I don't think old Ben wants anyone to come in."

"Maybe," Rudy agreed as he sealed up the box. "But you won't know unless you try knocking again."

Annie helped Rudy carry his things to his car. After saying good-bye, she stood in the parking lot thinking about what he'd said. The idea of trying to make friends with Ben Rowe made her cringe. Even if Rudy was right and Ben did want someone to try to befriend him, it sure wasn't going to be her. She already had two strikes against her. One more and she was out of the game.

She looked back at the doors to Shady Hills. Somewhere inside the nursing home, Ben Rowe was probably changing his pants and thinking about what a jerk Annie was. Could she really risk another encounter with him? Did she even want to? The answer to that question was a resounding no. But maybe Sophia had been right. Maybe Ben Rowe was a challenge she had to face.

Annie sighed. *Maybe you will strike out*, she thought. *But maybe you'll hit a home run instead.*

CHAPTER 6

Cooper checked her hair one final time in the side mirror of the blue Ford Explorer parked outside the restaurant. *I guess SUVs do come in handy sometimes*, she thought as she played with the carefully arranged spikes sticking up from her head. She'd gotten rid of the green color she'd put in as part of her Midsummer ritual costume, and now her hair was almost jet-black. It was the only color that would cover the green completely, and while it wasn't her favorite it would have to do either until her natural color grew back in or she could figure out what she wanted to do next. She was grateful that her hair was short and grew out quickly, so she wouldn't have long to wait.

She took another look at her outfit and then pushed open the door to the pizza place and walked in as if she hadn't just spent five minutes preparing her entrance. She scanned the booths, saw T.J. sitting at a table in the back, and made her way toward him.

"Hey," she said casually as she slid into the seat opposite him.

"You're a brunette now," T.J. commented. "Very Joan Jett."

Cooper snorted. "I wish I could play half as well as she can," she said.

"You can," T.J. said simply as he picked up the menu in front of him and opened it.

Cooper didn't respond, but inside she was glowing. T.J. was the first person who had ever complimented her on her guitar playing. It was one of the things she was most proud of, and to have him notice it made her feel good. She especially liked that he didn't make a big deal out of it. He wasn't trying to get in good with her, like some people did. He just liked the way she played.

"Have you talked to Jed or Mouse lately?" Cooper asked, wondering about the other two members of the band she and T.J. had put together.

T.J. shook his head. "Mouse is on vacation with her folks, and Jed is stuck in summer school," he said. "We won't be seeing much of him until fall."

Cooper nodded. That was fine with her. She liked Mouse and Jed, but the band was really hers and T.J.'s. They wrote the songs. The others just came to play. She was happy to have a couple of months just to write and try out new stuff.

"I think I'm going for the mushroom and spinach pizza," T.J. said, putting down his menu. "How about you?"

"Maybe the shrimp and pineapple," Cooper answered. "It sounds just weird enough to be good."

T.J. nodded. When the waitress came, they gave her their orders. Cooper looked around the restaurant, suddenly at a loss for anything to say. She'd never felt that way with T.J. before, and it bothered her.

"Last time I saw you, you were just about to go camping with your friends," T.J. said. "How'd that go?"

Cooper sighed. He was talking about the trip she had made with Annie and Kate to the Midsummer ritual. Had it really been that long since she'd seen T.J.? That seemed like forever ago. But she realized that it had only been a couple of weeks.

"It was okay," she said vaguely. "It wasn't really what I expected. I guess I'm just not the camping type."

She hoped that T.J. wouldn't ask her any more questions about the trip. She was afraid that would lead to talking about her involvement in Wicca. Several months before, when she had been going through all of the stuff surrounding the death of Elizabeth Sanger and her encounter with Elizabeth's ghost, Cooper'd been afraid that T.J. wouldn't want to be friends with her when he found out about what she could do. As it turned out, he had been very supportive of her at a time when many people weren't. But they'd never discussed those events, and they'd never talked about Cooper's interest in witchcraft.

Now she didn't want to discuss it. Once she would have liked more than anything to have a friend apart from Kate and Annie with whom she could be open about her interests. She'd thought for a while that that person might be T.J. Ironically, she now found herself hoping that he never brought it up. She didn't want it to be a big deal. For once in her life, she wanted to feel normal.

"So this concert should really kick," she said. "The last time I saw them, Mark dropped trou and mooned the audience."

T.J. smiled. "Maybe you should try that next time we play," he said, laughing.

Cooper laughed along with him. That was another thing she liked about T.J.—his sense of humor. He had a dryness to him that she found really refreshing. He didn't resort to stupid jokes like a lot of guys she knew did. In fact, he didn't talk all that much in general. *Except when he's with you*, she thought to herself. She'd never really thought about that before, but now that the thought had crossed her mind she realized that it was true. T.J. did talk more when they were alone together. She wondered why.

She looked at him sitting across from her. His red hair was, as usual, shaved down almost to the skin. The three earrings in his ear and the stud in his nose looked totally normal on him, not affected like they did on a lot of the kids who liked to think of themselves as punks or rocker types. T.J. always seemed to do things because he liked doing them, and not because anyone else said they were cool or because everyone was doing them. Cooper liked that.

Do you have a crush on this guy or what? she asked herself. The thought embarrassed her. She was the one who was always picking on Kate for being so boy crazy. She thought girls who drooled over guys were spritz-heads, brainless dolts who didn't have anything better to do than hang on their boyfriends' every word and sit at home waiting for them to call. She herself had never dated anyone, preferring to be by herself and pursue the things that interested her.

But T.J. liked the things that interested her. And she liked being around him. She could talk to him, at least when she wasn't scared of saying something stupid like she was now. But a boyfriend? She couldn't even imagine what that would be like.

The arrival of the pizza saved her from having to think about it anymore. As she and T.J. picked up their slices and started chewing, her thoughts turned to other things, namely Kate and Annie. She found herself wondering what they were doing. She hadn't called either of them in a long time, and she felt a little guilty about that. She'd almost picked up the phone on Tuesday night, but then she'd realized that they were probably at Crones' Circle with the rest of the study group.

Of the three of them, Cooper had always

thought that she was the one with the strongest ties to witchcraft. After all, her grandmother had been teaching her simple charms and spells when she was a little girl, even though Cooper hadn't realized what they were at the time. She was the one who had accused Kate of being afraid of what Wicca could do back when Kate had tried to run away from the group, and there had never been any doubt in her mind that she would be joining a coven as soon as her year and a day of study was completed. Why, she'd been one of the first ones to step up to the cauldron and claim her word of power during their dedication ceremony in April.

Connection. That had been her word. It was supposed to signify both the challenge of her journey that year as well as one of the gifts that would help her along the way. And at first her connections *had* helped her. Her friendship with Annie and Kate had brought a lot of good things to her life. Her connection to the women at Crones' Circle, and to the members of the various covens who participated in the rituals she attended, had taught her many things about magic and the Wiccan way. Even her connection to Elizabeth Sanger's ghost had been something she welcomed.

But those connections hadn't helped her during her ordeal on Midsummer Eve. If anything, her connections to the witch community had been severed that night when she'd run into those strange kids. After pretending to befriend her, they had turned on her. Even though they claimed it was all in fun, she hadn't had fun. She'd been frightened, and angry, and all they had succeeded in doing was showing her that sometimes connections couldn't be trusted.

But where did that leave Kate and Annie? Did cutting her ties to the Wiccan community mean she had to cut her ties to them as well? She didn't want to think that it did. But could she really still be friends with them in the way that they were all friends before? She wasn't sure that they could, and that made her sad.

"You look awfully serious all of a sudden," T.J. said, snapping her out of her thoughts. "Are you having vegetarian guilt over eating the shrimp?"

Cooper finished chewing the food in her mouth and swallowed. "Hardly," she said. "My rule is that I don't eat anything that has a face. I know technically shrimp have faces, but it's not quite the same as a cow or a pig or something with a snout. No, I was just thinking about some stuff that's been going on."

T.J. nodded. "Anything you want to talk about?"

Cooper was surprised. Besides Annie and Kate, and sometimes her parents, nobody ever asked her if she wanted to talk about what was bugging her. Usually, people stayed clear of her when she was in one of her moods. But here T.J. was going right into things.

"No," she said. "But thanks for asking."

"Any time," he said, shrugging as he picked up another piece of pizza and started eating.

They finished up, paid, and then walked a few doors down to the concert hall. People were already lined up outside waiting to get in, and Cooper saw some people she knew. She nodded to them as she and T.J. took their place in line. It felt good to be out doing something she liked, instead of sitting inside feeling sorry for herself. She hadn't been to a concert in a while, and she was ready to have some fun.

"Cooper," someone called out.

Cooper looked up and saw Sasha walking toward her, and her stomach churned. Like Cooper, Kate, and Annie, Sasha was involved in Wicca. Although she didn't participate in the weekly study group, she was living with Thea, one of the members of the coven that ran Crones' Circle. Sasha was a runaway, and Thea had recently been appointed her legal guardian. Cooper hadn't spoken to Sasha since deciding to leave the group, and she didn't know how much Sasha knew about what had happened to her and why she'd decided to stop coming to classes and rituals.

"Hi, Sasha," Cooper said nervously as the other girl stopped in front of her. "You look great."

It was true. Sasha did look great. Her once-scrawny frame had filled out, and she seemed happy and at ease.

"Thanks," replied Sasha. "Thea's cooking helps. It's really worked magic on me, if you know what I mean."

Cooper knew that this was a veiled reference to Sasha's involvement in the witch community and its transforming effect on her life. She was happy for her friend, but she wasn't about to get into a conversation about the Craft with her, especially not with T.J. there.

"Sasha, do you know T.J.?" she asked, looking for a diversion.

"I've seen you around," Sasha said.

"Me, too," T.J. answered. "Are you here for the show?"

Sasha shook her head. "Just passing through," she said. "But I'm glad I ran into you, Coop."

Cooper felt herself instinctively bristle at Sasha's use of the nickname she hated. Sasha knew she didn't like to be called Coop, but she did it to try to get a rise out of her. Cooper had given up telling her not to call her that.

"You heard about Kate, right?" Sasha continued.

Cooper shook her head. "No," she said. "I haven't talked to her in a while. Why? Has something happened?"

"Not to her," Sasha answered. "It's her aunt. She has cancer. Kate just found out. She was pretty bummed. I thought she would have told you."

"I've been kind of busy," Cooper said, but inside she was wondering the same thing Sasha was. Why hadn't Kate called her if something was wrong? *Probably because she thinks you don't want her to*, she thought guiltily.

"Well, she's taking it hard," said Sasha. "You should call her if you get a minute."

Cooper nodded. "Yeah," she said, "I will. Thanks for telling me."

"I should go," said Sasha. "You guys have a great time."

"Thanks," Cooper responded as Sasha waved and walked away.

"Wow," Cooper said, looking at T.J. "Cancer. That's rough. Poor Kate."

"If you want to go see her, that's okay," T.J. said. "We can skip the show."

Cooper shook her head. "No," she said. "That won't help anything. But I probably should go call her. I'll be right back."

She left T.J. in line and went to find a pay phone. There was one right down the block, and she was surprised to find it actually working when she picked up the receiver. She rummaged around in her pocket for the right change and dropped the coins into the coin slot. Then she began dialing Kate's number.

Wait a minute, she thought as she punched in the numbers. *What am I doing?* She hadn't talked to Kate in two weeks. Kate hadn't bothered to call *her* to tell her what had happened. What made her think Kate wanted to hear from her now?

She stood there for a moment, the phone in her hand, thinking about what she should do. Kate was her friend. Normally, Cooper would have been right there supporting her. But maybe Kate had stepped back for a reason. Maybe she didn't want Cooper involved in this.

Cooper hung up the phone and heard the coins clatter into the return slot. She fished inside and took them out, holding them in her palm for a minute as she considered making the call again. A big part of her wanted Kate to know that she was thinking of her. But maybe that connection, like some of the others in her life, needed to be cut. Maybe by leaving the group she'd gone too far away from Kate and the others in the Wiccan community and couldn't go back.

She put the coins in her pocket and walked back to T.J.

"Everything okay?" he asked.

"Yeah," Cooper lied. "Fine."

A minute later the doors opened and people began filing into the club. Cooper showed her license at the door and let the attendant snap a pink plastic bracelet around her wrist indicating that she wasn't yet old enough to buy alcohol. T.J. got one as well, and then they went inside, bypassing the table of overpriced T-shirts and other souvenirs.

Their seats were great, only a couple of rows from the stage and dead center. Cooper was amazed at how good they were.

"How did you get these tickets?" she asked T.J.

"A buddy of mine at a record store had them," he said. "It pays to have friends sometimes."

It sure does, Cooper thought. But what kind of

friend was she being, not even calling Kate? She didn't want to think about it.

Fortunately, she didn't have time to dwell on the subject. Not long after they sat down, the lights dimmed and the crowd leapt to its feet as Blink-182 took the stage. Cooper stood with them, enjoying the roar in her ears.

Mark and Tom launched into one of her favorite songs, "All the Small Things," while Curtis's tattooed arms beat the drums with a vengeance. Cooper sang along with the guys, screaming the words. There was so much cheering, and so many other people singing along as well, that she knew no one would hear her, or mind if they did. Everyone was there to have a great time, and that meant getting into things as much as possible.

For the next hour and a half she was on her feet, dancing and singing. From time to time she watched Tom's hands, trying to watch how he played his guitar and seeing if she could learn anything new. All other thoughts left her mind, and she found herself enveloped by the music. The familiar sense of peace filled her, the feeling that nothing else mattered except singing and playing. It was a magic all its own, and she welcomed it, embraced it. For the first time since that awful night in the woods, she was enjoying music again. The throbbing chords of Blink-182's songs had driven the eerie faerie melodies right out of her head.

When the show ended, after three raucous

encores during which the band did a bizarre but fantastic cover of the theme song from *Josie and the Pussycats*, Cooper and T.J. walked out of the theater and on to the street. Cooper was still pumped from the show, and she was thrilled that the concert had managed to knock the lingering taste of the faerie music out of her system.

"That was the best," she told T.J. as they walked toward the bus stop. "Thanks for asking me to go."

"Any time," he said.

They reached the bus stop and stood there, waiting for their respective buses. T.J. lived in a different part of town from Cooper, so they wouldn't be riding home together. When a bus pulled up, Cooper saw that it was hers, not T.J.'s. As the doors opened she turned to him.

"Thanks again," she said. "I really needed this."

T.J. smiled without saying anything. Then, before she realized what she was doing, Cooper leaned forward and kissed him. It was a quick kiss, but when she pulled back she was shocked at herself for doing it.

"I'm sorry," she said.

"Why?" T.J. asked.

Before he could say anything else Cooper turned and got onto the bus. As the doors closed and the bus pulled away, she looked out and saw T.J. watching her, a little smile on his face.

CHAPTER 7

"She's right in here," the nurse said to Kate, indicating a door on the left.

Kate paused a moment, the bouquet of flowers in her hands shaking as she tried to calm herself. *She's going to be fine*, she told herself. It was the mantra she'd been repeating ever since Thursday morning, when she and her mother had brought Aunt Netty to the hospital's cancer ward to begin a series of tests and treatment. That had only been a little more than thirty-six hours ago, surely not long enough for anything to have really happened yet.

Smiling broadly, Kate stepped into her aunt's room. Her mother was already there, sitting in a chair beside Aunt Netty's bed. Aunt Netty herself seemed to be asleep when Kate entered.

"How is she?" Kate asked her mother.

"The medication they're giving her makes her really tired," Mrs. Morgan answered. "She's been dozing on and off all day."

Kate looked at her sleeping aunt's face. Seeing

81

her like that, she looked almost healthy. Except for her missing hair, Kate would never have thought that something had gone terribly wrong inside her. But something had. Now they were trying to stop it. But would it work?

Aunt Netty's eyelids fluttered and opened. For a moment she seemed confused, her eyes glazed over and unfocused. But then she saw Kate standing there and she smiled.

"Hey, sweetie," she said, sounding a little hoarse. "Have I kept you waiting long?"

"I just got here," Kate said as her aunt struggled to sit up. Kate helped her, propping her up with some pillows. "How do you feel?"

"Like someone put me through the spin cycle," her aunt said. "What time is it?"

"Almost six," Kate told her. "Dinnertime."

Her aunt held up a hand. "Please," she said. "I can't even think about eating. Especially not hospital food."

"The medication makes her nauseated," Mrs. Morgan explained.

Kate pulled up a chair and sat next to her aunt. "What exactly are they doing?" she asked.

"Injecting me with poison," Aunt Netty responded. "Three times a day. It's supposed to knock out whatever is left of the cancer. Unfortunately, it seems to be knocking me out along with it."

"It's just about time for your next dose," Mrs. Morgan said.

As if on cue, a doctor appeared. She was young, Kate thought, and pretty. Her long blond hair hung past her shoulders, and she carried a file in her hand.

"Hi, Annette," she said, smiling. "How's it going?"

Aunt Netty laughed. "No one calls me Annette now that Mom is gone," she said. "Call me Netty. And I feel terrible."

"That's what I expected to hear," the doctor said.

"Kate, this is Dr. Pedersen," Mrs. Morgan said.

"Nice to meet you," the doctor said. "You must be the Kate I keep hearing about. Netty talks about you all the time, even when she's doing her treatments."

"Especially when I'm sitting there with a tube in my arm," said Kate's aunt. "It keeps my mind off of throwing up."

"Thanks, I think," said Kate.

There was a rattling as an aide appeared in the doorway of the room. He was a large, friendly looking guy, and when Aunt Netty saw him she smiled broadly.

"Hi, Nick," she said. "Have you come to take me away from all this?"

"You bet," Nick said, coming into the room and pulling a gurney behind him. "I even brought the stretch limo."

Nick put his hands behind Aunt Netty's back

and lifted her up. Kate was shocked to see how thin she looked in her nightgown as Nick carried her to the gurney and set her down. She'd lost a lot of weight, but Kate hadn't noticed it until now.

"I'll have her back by curfew," Nick said to Mrs. Morgan as he wheeled Aunt Netty out of the room.

"You'd better," joked Kate's mother. "I'll be waiting up."

When they were gone, Mrs. Morgan turned to the doctor. "How is she doing?" she asked.

The doctor sighed. "It hasn't been that long," she said. "We still don't know how the new chemotherapy is working."

"You look like there's something else," said Mrs. Morgan.

Dr. Pedersen opened the file she was holding. "I've been looking at the bone scan we did," she said. "There are some spots on a few of the bones. That suggests that the cancer is spreading."

"Can't you just take it out like you did the lump?" Kate asked anxiously. "Won't that make it go away?"

"Unfortunately, that's not how it works all of the time," the doctor replied. "Your aunt has a particularly aggressive type of cancer. It's metastasized, which means that it's spread from the site of the original tumor to other parts of her body."

"What parts?" asked Kate.

"First to her lymph nodes," the doctor said. "That was to be expected with this type of cancer.

But now it appears that it has spread. These spots on her bones are the first indications of that."

"Does she know?" Mrs. Morgan asked.

Dr. Pedersen shook her head. "I'm going to tell her as soon as this treatment is over. Then we'll have to decide what to do next."

No one said anything for a moment. Kate looked at her mother, who had a tired, sad expression on her face. Kate wondered what she was feeling, watching her little sister go through something so awful.

"I should get down there," said the doctor. "I'll be back up when Netty's treatment is over and I've had a chance to talk to her. Why don't the two of you go get something to eat. She'll probably be an hour or so."

"Thank you," Mrs. Morgan said as the doctor left. Then she turned to Kate. "You heard the doctor," she said. "Let's go find something to eat."

Kate stood up and followed her mother out of the room, walking to the elevator. Neither of them said anything as they waited for the doors to open, or on the way down to the first floor and the hospital cafeteria. As they wound their way through the line, looking at the unappetizing offerings, Kate wanted desperately to ask the question that was weighing heavily on her mind, but she couldn't bring herself to do it.

It wasn't until they were seated at one of the little plastic tables, chewing their cardboard-tasting sandwiches, that Kate finally asked, "Is Aunt Netty dying?"

Her mother put down her food, wiped her mouth, and looked at Kate. "I don't know," she said. "I honestly don't know."

Kate choked back a little sob. If her mother really believed that Netty would be okay, she would have said so. But she hadn't, which made Kate think that even her mother expected the worst, even if she wouldn't say it. It's what she herself suspected, but it was worse knowing that her mother, the person who had always comforted her and told her that everything would be all right, was also worried. As a little girl, when she was frightened by thunderstorms, it was her mother who'd soothed her and told her stories about how the scary sounds were just the sky laughing. When she fell and scraped her knee, or had a bee sting, she'd trusted that her mother would make her feel better.

But now Mrs. Morgan couldn't do anything to make Kate feel better. She couldn't make Aunt Netty's cancer go away. She couldn't stop the hurting. She couldn't tell Kate that it would all be better in the morning. All she could do was sit there beneath the ugly fluorescent lights and tell Kate that one of the people she loved most in the world might be dying.

Kate didn't know what to say. She looked at her mother, who had put her hands over her eyes. When she removed them, Kate could see tears sliding down her face. Her mother sighed deeply, as if trying to keep from crying, and used her napkin to wipe her eyes.

"I'm sorry," she said.

"For what?" Kate asked, about to cry herself.

"For not telling you sooner," said her mother. "We didn't want to worry you. Netty thought the first tumor was the only one. We didn't want to scare anyone by saying anything. That was wrong."

"No," Kate said. "It wasn't wrong. And I'm not mad."

She stood up and went to her mother. Leaning down, she put her arms around her and hugged her tightly. As she did, she felt her mother begin to shake. She was crying, openly now, and Kate felt warm tears falling on her arms. She'd rarely seen her mother cry, and she knew that what was happening to Netty must be tearing her apart.

"I love you, Mom," Kate said. "Don't worry. Everything will be okay."

Their roles had reversed. Now it was Kate comforting her mother, who trembled with fear and sadness. She felt her mother's hand reach up to clasp her own, and they remained like that for several minutes as her mother released the unhappiness inside of her. It broke Kate's heart to feel her sobbing, but at the same time she felt a kind of strength filling her, the strength that came from wanting to protect someone she cared for from any more pain.

"She's my baby sister," Mrs. Morgan said, her

voice choking. "It's not supposed to be like this. I'm supposed to be able to help her, and I can't. I can't do anything."

Kate stroked her mother's hair gently as if she was the child and Kate was the mother. She kept saying "It will be all right. It will be all right." But she wasn't sure she believed it. How could it be all right when the cancer was destroying Aunt Netty's body at such a furious rate? How could it be all right when her mother, who was always the one to believe that things would work out, was sobbing in her arms? She didn't know, but she kept saying it anyway, as if repeating it over and over would make it true.

Eventually, her mother's breathing evened out as she stopped crying. She let go of Kate's hand and patted it gently. Then she dabbed at her face with the napkin and sighed.

"We should go back upstairs," she said. "Netty should be back by now."

Kate looked at her mother's face. Her eyes were red from crying. "Maybe we should wait a minute," she suggested.

"Am I a mess?" asked Mrs. Morgan.

"A little," Kate said, and both of them laughed tentatively.

Her mother looked at her and smiled. "Thank you," she said. "I know this must be really hard for you."

"Usually, I'm the one who's a mess," Kate replied.

"Well, now you know how I feel when you are," said her mother.

"It's not a nice feeling," Kate admitted. "I don't really know how I'm supposed to feel about all of this. I want to be brave, for you and Aunt Netty. And I want to be sad, for me. But mostly it just feels weird. This is the kind of thing that happens to other people, or to people in movies or something. But now that it's really happening, it's not at all like I would expect it to be."

"I know what you mean," her mother answered. "When Netty first called me and told me about the tumor, my first thought was that it was all a joke, or that somehow it wasn't her and it was someone who dialed a wrong number. I just couldn't bring myself to believe what she was saying. It was like she was talking about somebody else, somebody I didn't really know and who just happened to have the same name that she did. Then I remembered the time when Kyle got hurt playing ice hockey. Your father called me from the hospital to say that he might have some spinal cord injury because he wasn't moving and couldn't feel his legs. I didn't believe him. I kept telling him that he must be mistaken, that it must be some other boy and not Kyle because that couldn't happen to my little boy. It wasn't until I was at the hospital and saw him for myself that it really hit me."

"But Kyle was okay," Kate said. "Maybe the same thing will happen with Aunt Netty."

Her mother smiled. "Maybe," she said, but she didn't sound at all sure of herself.

They carried their trays to the garbage can and left the cafeteria. As they walked back to the elevators, Mrs. Morgan took Kate's hand.

"I know I tell you that I love you a lot," she said. "You and Kyle. And I'm sure sometimes it just sounds like something to say when you leave for school or go out with your friends. But I want you to know that every time I say it I mean it with all my heart."

"I know you do," Kate replied. "And I mean it, too."

"No matter what happens to Netty, she loves you," Mrs. Morgan continued. "You mean a lot to her, and it means a lot to her that you're here with her during all of this. She pretends to be fine, but I know she's scared."

Kate nodded. She couldn't say anything. If she did she would start crying again, and she wanted to look as normal as possible when she went in to see her aunt.

They rode the elevator to the third floor and got off. When they walked into Aunt Netty's room, Dr. Pedersen was sitting beside her bed. Netty had a stunned look on her face, and Kate knew that the doctor had told her the news that her cancer had spread to her bones. Still, when Netty saw them in the doorway she managed a smile.

"I hope you didn't eat all the creamed corn,"

she said. "I ordered extra for dinner tonight."

"No, we left some for you," Mrs. Morgan said.

"I was just going over Netty's lab reports with her. Everything's going right—except we don't have any indication of this round of chemo's effectiveness on the cancer. We have to wait and see," Dr. Pedersen said.

"But you can't just do nothing!" Kate burst out, sounding angrier than she meant to because she was frustrated. "What good are all these different treatments if you can't depend on them?"

"I understand how you feel, Kate," said the doctor kindly. "Believe me, I get just as frustrated waiting for results. But there are limits, even in medicine, and we have to work with them."

"I only have to do these treatments for another few weeks, Kate," her aunt said. "Then Dr. Pedersen will be able to give us an update."

"But that could be too la—" Kate started to say, stopping herself when she realized how awful it sounded.

There was silence for a minute as they all tried very hard not to look at one another. Then Aunt Netty spoke. "It will take more than a few days to get rid of me," she said.

Kate started to apologize, but her aunt stopped her. "It's okay," she said. "Do you think I haven't thought about that? Not saying it isn't going to make it go away."

Dr. Pedersen stood up. "I know none of this is

easy," she said. "But Netty is right; not talking doesn't help. If any of you have any questions, please don't hesitate to ask me. I'll tell you everything I can."

"Thanks, Doc," Netty said, coughing a little bit. "So, are we on for tomorrow morning? I can't wait for another dose of that stuff you're pumping into me."

"Keep it up," the doctor said teasingly. "I'll have the techs use the really big needles if you give me any trouble."

Kate marveled at how the two of them could sound so relaxed about everything. If she were the one in the bed instead of Aunt Netty, she would have been hysterical. She just knew it. But her aunt was acting as if this were an everyday occurrence in her life.

The doctor left, and Mrs. Morgan went to stand beside Netty. Kate took the opportunity to follow the doctor out into the hall.

"Dr. Pedersen," she said, jogging after the retreating figure. "Can I ask you something?"

The doctor stopped. "Sure, Kate. What is it?"

"Well, I was just wondering if there isn't anything we can do. I mean, anything I can do. To help. I feel really useless right now."

The doctor smiled. "You're doing exactly what's best for your aunt," she said. "You're here with her. Leave the rest to me and the wonders of modern science."

"But isn't there anything else?" Kate said. She knew it sounded childish, but she didn't know any other way to vent her frustration.

Dr. Pedersen looked thoughtful. "You can pray for her," she said.

"Pray?" said Kate.

The doctor nodded her head.

"My job is to know the best way to treat your aunt medically," the doctor explained. "But medicine isn't always the only way to help someone. There's been a lot of research done that shows that patients who have a strong connection to spirituality often respond more positively to treatment when there's a faith aspect to it."

"You mean they believe they'll get better because they pray?" Kate said.

"Something like that," said Dr. Pedersen. "If people think there's something greater than themselves, or greater than medicine, helping them, it might have an effect on the healing process. I know it seems like the medical establishment knows everything about how the body works, but the fact is we don't. People die who should easily get well. People live who should by all scientific reasoning be dead. There's a link between the mind and the body that we simply don't understand fully."

"I don't know," Kate said. "I don't think Aunt Netty is all that religious."

"It's just a suggestion," the doctor replied.

"Well, thanks," Kate said. "I'll think about it."

The doctor left, and Kate walked back to her aunt's room. Before she entered, she paused. What Dr. Pedersen said had given her an idea. Maybe she was right. Maybe there *was* something Kate could do. But it was something a little different from what the doctor suggested.

A ritual, she thought suddenly. *I could do a ritual.*

CHAPTER 8

Annie clutched the package beneath her arm tightly. She still wasn't sure that she was doing the right thing. But she'd made up her mind to do it, and she was going to go through with it, even if it made everything worse. *As if that's even possible*, she thought as she walked down the hall toward Ben Rowe's room.

Part of her hoped that the old man wouldn't be in there. That way she could just leave the package and let him find it on his own. But she knew that giving it to him in person would be better, if not easier. She'd been thinking about it most of the night, going over and over in her head all of the reasons for not doing what she'd decided to do. She'd almost convinced herself to forget about it, too. Then, as she was walking out the door to go to the bus that morning, she'd seen the package sitting on the kitchen counter where she'd put it and had picked it up.

She stopped outside Ben's room, listening for

any sounds that would indicate that he was inside. When she didn't hear anything, she let out a little sigh of relief. Maybe she wouldn't have to face him after all. She could leave the package and maybe come back later, after he'd had a chance to open it.

But when she stepped into the room she saw that he was there after all. He was sitting in the chair next to the room's one window. The blinds had been pulled up just enough for him to look out, and he was gazing off into the distance with a faraway look on his face. He didn't look up, and Annie wondered if he even knew someone had come in.

She cleared her throat to indicate that she was there, and Ben turned his head. "What do you want?" he barked.

Annie felt her resolve waning. Ben clearly knew who she was, and he didn't want her in his room. She couldn't blame him. She was tempted to just put the package on his dresser and leave. But then she stopped herself.

"I came to bring you something," she said, her voice unsteady.

"I don't want anything," Ben said simply. "Just leave me alone."

He turned and resumed staring out the window, clearly thinking that he had dismissed Annie. But she didn't leave, even though she wanted to. Instead, she stepped closer to him and held out the package.

"Please," she said. "I want you to have this."

Ben glanced at the paper bag in her hands. "I don't want it," he said simply.

"You don't even know what it is," Annie said.

"I don't care what it is," the old man answered. "I don't want anything from you."

Annie was getting frustrated. She was trying to do something nice, and Ben wasn't letting her. She could understand his being upset with her, and even wanting to be alone, but she couldn't understand why he was being so rude.

She looked around and saw the picture frame she'd broken sitting on the dresser. Ben had put the photo back in the frame, but the glass was missing and the frame was cracked. It listed to one side, as if it might topple over at any moment.

Annie opened the bag and reached inside, pulling out the frame she had picked up at a store the night before. It was a beautiful wooden frame, and she'd chosen it because she thought it would show off the black-and-white photo beautifully. Now, as she placed it on the dresser, she saw that she'd made a good choice.

"What is that?" Ben snapped.

"It's a frame to replace the one I broke," Annie said as she picked up the old frame and slipped off the back. She knew that she was risking making the old man angry again by touching his photo, but she didn't have anything to lose, so she continued, sliding the picture into the new frame and snapping the back on.

"There," she said, holding it out to Ben. "I'm sorry."

Ben Rowe looked at the photograph in Annie's hand, eyeing it suspiciously. But he didn't make any move to take it from her. Annie stood there for a moment, waiting for him to do something. Then, when he didn't, she put the photograph back on the dresser and turned away.

"I hope you like it," she said as she walked toward the door.

"Wait," Ben said gruffly.

Annie stopped and turned back to him, wondering what he wanted. Again, though, he didn't say anything. He just stared at the picture on the bureau.

"If you don't like it I can take it back," Annie said. "I just thought you might like a new frame. That one was pretty beat up, and from the looks of the photo it's one that's special to you, so I thought it should go in something nice."

The old man remained silent. *Why did he tell me to wait if he's just going to sit there glaring at me?* Annie wondered. She just couldn't figure out Ben Rowe at all.

"That's me and my brother," Ben said, breaking the silence.

"I thought it might be," replied Annie. "I saw the inscription on the back."

For the first time ever Annie saw the man give something like a smile. But almost as quickly as it appeared it was gone, replaced by the familiar stern expression.

"That was taken in 1942," Ben continued after a moment. "We were both on leave from the service. I was in the army and Tad was in the air force."

"You fought in the war?" Annie asked.

Ben nodded. "I carried that picture all over Europe with me," he said. "It was my good luck charm."

"No wonder it's so wrinkled," Annie said, forgetting that she was speaking out loud and then feeling embarrassed about having said anything.

But Ben didn't seem to notice. "That picture was in my shirt pocket for three years," he said. "I looked at it every day. It kept me going when I didn't want to."

He stopped talking and looked down at his hands.

"What happened to your brother?" she asked.

"He was killed," Ben answered, speaking slowly, as if saying the words hurt his mouth. "In France during a nighttime raid on the Germans in Paris. His plane was shot down."

Annie didn't know what to say. Telling the man she was sorry didn't seem appropriate. So she remained quiet.

"That's what happens in wartime," he continued. "People die. We all knew that. I watched many of my friends die, sometimes two or three of them a day. I waited to be killed every second I was out there. That's what soldiers do."

"But those people weren't your brother," Annie said.

Ben looked up at her. But this time he didn't look angry. He looked sad. "No," he said. "They weren't my brother."

"You must miss him," said Annie.

Ben nodded. "Yes," he said. "It's been almost sixty years since that photo was taken. Sixty years since I last spoke to him. But I do miss him. I miss him every day."

Annie felt a great sadness well up inside her. Ben Rowe didn't seem like an angry old man to her anymore. He was just someone who missed his brother.

"Do you have any other family?" she asked.

"No," Ben said. "We were the only two. I never married."

Annie wondered how Ben had come to live at Shady Hills and what he had done with his life before that. There were all kinds of questions flying around in her head. But one question stood out above them all.

"What did he mean about the fender?" she asked.

Ben Rowe laughed. The sound surprised Annie. It was almost creaky, as if the old man's vocal cords weren't accustomed to making such a sound. But it also filled her with a rush of gladness. She'd broken through Ben's shell. She'd gotten him to talk to her, and that felt wonderful.

"The fender," Ben said, slapping his hands on his thighs in delight. "I hadn't thought about that in many, many years. I had a car then, a 'forty-one Ford, if I remember correctly. Tad begged me to let him drive it. I could never say no to him, so I let him. Of course the first thing he did was run it into an old apple tree while trying to get out of the driveway. I could have killed him, but he was laughing so hard I couldn't be mad."

Ben stood up, walked to the dresser, and picked up the photograph. His fingers stroked the wood of the new frame. Then he looked at Annie.

"Thank you," he said quietly.

Annie smiled. "You're welcome," she said. "Like I said, I felt bad about breaking the other one."

"This is the only photo I have left of Tad," Ben said.

"I noticed that you don't really have a lot of personal stuff in here," Annie commented hesitantly. She didn't want to risk making Ben Rowe angry, not after she'd managed to finally get things off to a pretty good start.

Ben snorted. "Why bother?" he said. "It's just a room."

"But you have to live in it," Annie protested. "You should fix it up a little."

"I was never very good at that kind of thing," Ben said.

Annie opened the paper bag again. "Well, luckily I am," she said. "I got you something else."

Ben watched warily as Annie pulled her second surprise out of the bag. She'd been hanging on to it, in case things went badly. But she seemed to be on a roll, so she figured she could chance it.

"I think these are a good start," she said, holding up a pair of curtains made out of a pretty blue material. She'd found them at the store and picked them up on impulse.

"This place needs some cheering up," she told Ben as she walked over to his window. Pulling the blinds up, she let some of the bright sunlight in. Almost immediately the space felt lighter and cozier. Ben watched her as she stood on his chair and took down the empty curtain rod that hung above the window.

"You don't have to do that," he said.

"I know I don't have to," Annie answered as she slipped the first curtain over the rod. "But I want to."

"Why?" Ben asked.

It was a good question. Annie had asked herself the same thing over and over as she'd made her plans. Why was she so interested in making friends with Ben Rowe, or at least getting him to talk to her? It would have been easy to just ignore him, to let him keep on being angry and unpleasant. But for some reason she'd felt the need to take him on as a kind of project.

"I know what it's like to be lonely," she said, hanging the second curtain and stepping off the chair.

She turned to see Ben's reaction to the drapes. They really did give the room a whole different appearance. The old man was looking at them with an unreadable expression on his face. Did he hate them? Annie couldn't tell.

"My parents died," she told him. "When I was little. I know how that feels."

"It doesn't go away," he said suddenly. "The pain. It changes as time goes by, but it's always there. People like to tell you that it goes away, but it doesn't. It's like part of you died with the person who's gone, and you don't get that back."

He seemed to be talking as much to himself as he was to Annie. She knew what he meant. He was right; the pain hadn't gone away for her either. It had grown less, but it was still there.

"You came here because of them, didn't you?" Ben asked her.

Annie nodded. She hadn't told anybody her real reason for volunteering at the home, but he had guessed it. She'd come there because she wanted to understand. She wanted to understand what happened to people as they prepared to die. She wanted to look at something that people usually tried hard to avoid. She'd been avoiding it all of her life, ever since the night the fire had claimed her parents. Now she was trying to face it in her own way.

"The curtains look nice," Ben said, as if their previous conversation were at an end.

"Yeah," Annie said. "I think they look good. And if you want to, we can do some other stuff, too."

Ben looked at her. "You're quite a girl," he said.

Annie laughed. "Coming from you, I think that's the best compliment I could ask for," she said.

"But you're not very good at magic tricks," the old man added.

"Just be glad I wasn't trying to saw you in half," Annie shot back.

"Annie, could you come help me in the office for a minute?"

Mrs. Abercrombie was standing in the doorway. She was looking from Annie to the curtains to Ben with a puzzled look on her face.

"Can't you see we're talking?" Ben snapped at the nurse, suddenly his grouchy old self again.

"It's okay," Annie said. "We're done. I'll come back later, Mr. Rowe."

As she walked out of the room, she caught Ben's eye and he winked at her. Annie smiled, silently laughing at their private joke. She knew he had put on his tough guy act for Mrs. Abercrombie. But she also knew that she had made a new friend. *Home run*, she thought as she went into the hallway.

"Don't tell me you willingly went into the lion's den," the nurse said as they walked away together.

"It wasn't so bad," Annie answered. "I took a whip and a chair with me."

* * *

Later that night, Annie sat in her room, talking to Kate on the phone.

"She looks terrible," Kate said. She'd just finished telling Annie what had happened at the hospital that afternoon.

"And you think doing a ritual might help?" Annie asked.

"I don't know," Kate said. "I don't think it can hurt, right? We're always talking about how magic is energy and how it can be used to change things. Why couldn't we use it to help heal someone? When I was doing that report for class I read a lot about how early witches were really people who knew how to heal."

"What do you have in mind?" Annie asked her friend.

"I'm not sure," answered Kate. "I haven't had a lot of time to think about it. We just got home a little while ago. I'm going to think about it tonight and come up with something. But I thought maybe we could get together tomorrow night at your house and do it. Is that okay?"

"Sure," Annie said. "Just let me know if you need me to get anything or do anything. Do you think we should talk to Sophia or Archer about this?"

"I don't think so," Kate replied. "It's not like that first time, when we didn't really know what we were doing. Besides, it's not really a spell or anything. I think we're okay on our own."

Annie paused, unsure of whether or not to say what she was thinking. "What about Cooper?" she asked finally.

Kate sighed. "I thought about that, too. I don't know. She's been so distant lately, and she said she doesn't want to be involved in anything to do with Wicca right now."

"This is sort of different, though," Annie countered. "It's not like it's with a group or anything. It's just us."

"It would be nice to have her there," Kate admitted. "I guess I could ask her."

They talked for a few more minutes and then hung up. Annie sat on her bed, thinking about what was happening. She looked at the picture hanging on the wall across from her bed. It was one her mother had done. Her aunt had found it in a storage space while looking for paintings to use in a show of Chloe Crandall's work that she had arranged as a surprise for Annie the month before. The painting depicted Annie as a little girl looking out a window at the moon. Whenever Annie looked at it she felt happy, as if her mother were still there, holding her in her arms.

She didn't want Kate to lose her aunt. She knew her friend was afraid that that's exactly what was going to happen. Even worse, she had time to think about it. When Annie's parents had died, it had been unexpected and sudden. The shock had been terrible, and the pain almost unbearable. She imagined it had been the same for Ben Rowe, losing his brother the way he had. Neither of them had gotten a chance to say good-bye to the people they loved.

But Kate was watching her aunt die before her eyes. Annie wasn't sure if that was easier or harder. It gave Kate a chance to say everything she wanted to. But it also meant that she had to spend every day not knowing if it was going to be the last one they had together. Would it have made anything easier if *she* had known that her parents were going to die? She didn't know.

She heard laughter coming up the stairs from the kitchen. Her aunt and her little sister were doing something there. Annie smiled at the sounds of their voices. They sounded so happy. Meg's high-pitched shrieks were followed by her aunt's rolling laughter, as if they were chasing one another around the room. Despite her concern for Kate, Annie couldn't help but be glad that she had people she loved around her.

"Hey," she called, jumping off the bed and heading for the door. "Stop having so much fun without me."

CHAPTER 9

"Hello?" Cooper said, picking up the phone next to her bed. She wondered who would be calling her at nine o'clock on a Saturday morning.

"Hi," said Kate. "It's Kate."

There was an awkward silence as Cooper hesitated. She didn't know what to say next.

"I've been meaning to call you," she said finally. "Sasha told me about your aunt."

"That's sort of why I'm calling," Kate said. "I was wondering if you could help me out."

"Sure," Cooper said instantly, relieved that Kate didn't seem to be angry with her. "What do you need?"

"Annie and I are doing a ritual," she said. She stopped, letting the words sink in.

"A ritual?" Cooper said doubtfully.

"Yeah," Kate continued. "At her house tonight. It's to help my aunt. Well, I hope it will help her. I don't really know. But at this point it can't hurt."

"Is she that bad?" Cooper asked, avoiding Kate's question.

"It's not good," answered Kate. "The cancer is in her bones."

Cooper closed her eyes and pressed her hand to her forehead. She could tell Kate wasn't doing well herself. Her friend's normally cheerful voice sounded almost drugged, as if she hadn't been sleeping much.

"So what do you think?" Kate said. "Will you come?"

Cooper let out a long breath. "I don't know, Kate," she said. "You know I'm done with all of that."

"I know," Kate said, "but this isn't really like doing something with a lot of people. It's just me and Annie."

"I just don't think I'd be any use," Cooper said. "You know you have to be in the right frame of mind for this stuff to work right. I don't want to bring any negative energy to it."

There was more silence as Kate didn't respond. Then she said, "The three of us have done some really great work together. Your energy was part of that. In fact, if it weren't for you we would probably never have gotten together."

"That was different," Cooper protested. "I was really into all of it then. I'm not now. I know you and Annie don't understand what happened to me, but it wasn't a lot of fun. I don't want to get involved with that kind of thing again."

"I think you're blaming everything to do with Wicca for what one group of people did to you," Kate said.

"Maybe I am," Cooper told her. "But that's not the whole thing. It's about magic, Kate, and about what happens when it gets out of control. Remember what happened with you and Scott?"

"But I didn't know what I was doing!" countered Kate. "Now I do. And so does Annie. And so do you. It's not going to get out of control, I promise."

"Things were supposed to be in control during the Litha ritual, too," Cooper said. "But something went wrong. Those people invited the faerie magic into the woods and somehow it took over."

Talking about what had happened to her was making Cooper upset. She wanted to help Kate, but she knew she wouldn't be any good in a ritual with her and Annie. Her heart just wasn't in it anymore.

"I'm sorry, Kate," she said. "I really am. I know how much you love your aunt. And I think your doing a ritual with Annie is a good idea. But not with me involved in it."

"I guess if that's really how you feel there's nothing I can say that will change your mind," Kate said softly. "You never listen to anyone else anyway."

Those words stung, and for a second Cooper almost shot back with something equally cutting. But then she remembered who she was talking to, and she kept quiet.

"Good luck, Kate," she said. "Even though you probably don't believe it, I'll be thinking about you tonight. I hope it all works out."

She hung up before Kate could say anything else. Leaning back against her pillows, she closed her eyes. *Well*, she thought, *I guess that's it*. She was sure that she had just ruined any chance of keeping Kate as her friend. Maybe Annie, too. Why would they want to remain friends with her when she couldn't even help them out? But she knew that she couldn't.

The phone rang again and she picked it up, thinking it might be Kate calling back.

"Hey," said T.J. "I hope I didn't wake you up or anything."

"No," Cooper replied. "I've been up for a while."

She hadn't spoken to T.J. since the night of the Blink-182 concert. *The night you kissed him*, she reminded herself. She still couldn't believe that she'd done it.

"I guess I should apologize about the other night," she said quickly.

"Why?" T.J. said. "Your singing wasn't that bad."

"I meant about the other thing," Cooper said. "You know, when I sort of kissed you."

"Oh, that," said T.J. "Apology accepted."

"I don't know what happened," continued Cooper. "I was having such a great time, and I just sort of did it."

"Yeah, I was kind of surprised," T.J. said. "I

111

thought I would be the one to do it first."

"I'm just glad you're not ang— What did you say?" Cooper asked, shocked.

"I said I was surprised," T.J. repeated. "I'd been trying to think of a way I could do it first. But you beat me to it."

"Oh," Cooper said, dumbfounded. "You mean you *wanted* me to do it?"

"The thought had crossed my mind," T.J. said. "Is that okay?"

"Yeah," answered Cooper. "I mean, sure. If that's what you want."

"Then I guess it's okay with you if we do it again sometime," said T.J.

Cooper was speechless. Was T.J. telling her that he wanted to go out with her? *Of course he is, you idiot,* she berated herself. She had to think about that for a minute. Her and T.J. A couple. The idea was strange, but it made her excited as well.

"You still there?" she heard him ask.

"Yeah," Cooper said. "I just spaced for a minute there. So let me get this straight—are we going out here?"

"I don't know," T.J. replied. "I mean, we've only had one date, and you pulled a Cinderella at the end of it. I think we need to have another one and see how it goes."

"Thursday night was a date?" said Cooper.

T.J. sighed. "Well, I guess not since you didn't seem to know it was."

Cooper laughed, feeling like an idiot. "I'm sorry," she said. "It's just that it didn't occur to me. I'm not really all that good at this kind of thing."

"Well, you seem to have the kissing thing down okay," T.J. told her. "At least that's how it seems from the little bit of it I've experienced."

Cooper knew she was blushing, something she never did. What was it about T.J. that disarmed her so much? She'd never known a guy like him before. Usually, she could cut guys down with one comment. But he was the one putting her on the defensive. Not in a bad way, but in a way that made her feel like she was finally talking to someone who could keep up with her.

"Maybe we should try this whole first date thing again," Cooper suggested. "What are you up to today?"

"I was going to suggest we go for a sail," T.J. told her.

"A sail?" said Cooper. "As in on a boat?"

"That's it," T.J. said. "Are you up for it?"

"You have a boat?" Cooper asked.

"Wait until you see it," answered T.J. "You'll love it. Meet me at the wharf at eleven, okay?"

"Okay," Cooper said. "I'll see you then."

She hung up and sat in her bed, thinking. She had a boyfriend. Well, a sort-of boyfriend. She'd never had one before. She wasn't sure how she was supposed to feel now that she and T.J. were apparently an item. What did girls with boyfriends do?

She thought about Kate and Tyler, holding hands during class and making eyes at one another. Would she have to do that? *I can't,* she told herself. *It would be too much.*

Suddenly, she missed Annie and Kate. If they were around she could talk to them about all of this. As much as she teased Kate about being too into boys, Cooper had always secretly admired the fact that Kate could handle the whole dating thing with relative ease. She would know just what to do. *But you basically just told her you couldn't be friends with her,* she reminded herself. *So it looks like you're on your own.*

She got up and went to the bathroom to shower. When she was done she dressed and went downstairs to the kitchen, where her mother was just finishing her second cup of coffee and starting to look at least partially coherent.

"Morning, honey," her mother said sleepily.

"Good morning," Cooper answered. She poured herself a big glass of grapefruit juice and sat down across from her mother.

"Um, can I ask you something?" she began nervously.

"As long as it doesn't involve me having to think or do math, then yes," said Mrs. Rivers.

"Why does anyone date?" said Cooper.

Her mother sighed. "Is this a trick question?" she asked.

Cooper shook her head. "No," she said. "I'm

serious. What's the point of dating people, at least when you're in high school? It's not like you're really going to marry that person, right? You're both going to go on to college and change and then probably break up. So if it's doomed from the beginning, what's the point?"

"Did your father put you up to this?" asked her mother. "It's the sort of thing he would ask."

"I'm serious," said Cooper. "Why date anyone when you know it isn't going to go anywhere?"

"For the practice, I guess," answered Mrs. Rivers. When she saw her daughter giving her a stern look, she continued. "I'm serious. You date when you're young because it teaches you how to be in a relationship. I agree with you that it isn't easy. But it's what we do. If everyone waited until the last second and just got married, we'd make a mess of it."

"Most people seem to anyway," suggested Cooper.

"Well, yes," agreed her mother. "A lot of them do. But my point is that if you date when you're, well, your age, then you get a lot of those mistakes out of the way early on."

Suddenly, she stopped talking and eyed her daughter in a different way. "Why are you asking me this?"

Cooper took a long drink of juice. "No reason," she said innocently. "I was just thinking about it."

"Give me a break," said Mrs. Rivers. "I haven't

been married to one of the best lawyers in Beecher Falls for twenty years for nothing. I know when someone's trying to pull one over on me, Cooper Rivers, and that's what *you're* trying to do. Spill it."

Cooper groaned. She and her mother had never been the kind to have heart-to-heart talks like other mothers and daughters seemed to. In fact, they seemed to disagree about almost everything. But her mother had her, and Cooper knew she couldn't bluff her way out of it this time.

"There's just this guy," she said.

"Not that tall redheaded boy with the thing in his nose?" her mother said.

Cooper rolled her eyes. "His name is T.J."

"T.J.," her mother said, as if trying out how it sounded. "So it is him?"

"Yes," Cooper said. "I guess we're kind of dating. I mean, we're going to. We apparently had a date the other night when we went to the concert, but I didn't know it."

Her mother smiled. "You're so like your father it isn't funny. He didn't know we were on a date the first time either."

"Really?" said Cooper. "You mean I'm not the only one who's dating challenged?"

Mrs. Rivers shook her head. "It wasn't until our third date that he realized what was going on," she said. "He thought the first two were just study sessions for our sophomore philosophy class. I had to tell him that I wasn't even in the same class that he was and that I'd borrowed the books from my roommate."

"Even I'm not that bad," Cooper remarked.

"So, tell me more about this guy," her mother said. "What's he like?"

"Can we talk about it later?" Cooper asked. "I'm supposed to meet him soon for our first official date."

"Fine," said Mrs. Rivers. "But I want all the details when you get back."

"I'll keep notes," Cooper joked, getting up and putting her glass in the sink.

Half an hour later she got off the bus at the wharf. T.J. was standing there, waiting for her.

"So where's this boat?" Cooper asked.

T.J. pointed to the end of the dock. "Right there," he said.

Cooper looked. "But that's the whale watch tour boat," she said.

"I didn't say it was *my* boat," said T.J. "I just said it was a boat."

Cooper punched him playfully in the arm. "You are such a freak," she said.

"What? You don't like whales?" said T.J.

"I've actually never seen one," Cooper said.

"Then let's go look for some," suggested T.J. "The next tour starts in twenty minutes."

They went and purchased tickets, then boarded the boat. They found seats on the top deck, in a secluded corner where they could look out over the railing. As the boat pulled away from the dock and headed out into the open water, Cooper felt herself relaxing.

"I do this about once a month," T.J. told her.

"Really?" said Cooper. "Do you like whales that much?"

T.J. laughed. "It's a couple of hours that I can be alone," he said. "And it's so beautiful out here. Sometimes I forget how pretty Beecher Falls is."

Cooper gazed out over the gently rolling water. To one side she could see the shoreline with its beaches and the mountains in the distance. It really *was* gorgeous.

"This feels kind of weird," T.J. said.

"What does?" asked Cooper.

"Being here with you," he explained.

"Thanks a lot," she exclaimed.

"I didn't mean it that way," T.J. said. "I mean, up until now we've just been friends, you know? I'm not exactly sure what we're supposed to do now."

"I know what you mean," agreed Cooper. "It's a little awkward."

"Maybe we need to do something to get over it," suggested T.J.

"Like what?" asked Cooper. "Sign a contract or carve our initials into this bench or something?"

"I was thinking more along the lines of this," said T.J. as he leaned over and kissed her.

This time Cooper didn't pull away. Instead, she slid her arm around T.J.'s waist and held on to him, kissing him back. She felt the warmth of his skin against hers, and the pressure of his mouth where it touched her lips. She could tell that he was nervous, too, and that made her like him even more.

When they finally pulled apart, she said, "I know that helped *me* a lot. How about you?"

"I think I'm over it, too," he said. "This transition from friend to boyfriend might not be as hard as I thought."

They sat, holding hands and watching the surface of the ocean as the boat moved gently through the water. The July afternoon was hot, and Cooper soaked up the sun's warmth eagerly. It felt good to be away from solid ground, surrounded by the ocean. Even though there were other people onboard, she felt as if she and T.J. were on their own floating island.

"Look," said T.J., suddenly leaping up and going to the railing.

Cooper followed him, looking where he was pointing. As she did she saw the surface of the water break and a huge dark shape rise from it. It was a whale. Its black skin was covered with large patches of barnacles, and the surface of it shimmered wetly in the sun. Then another, smaller whale appeared next to the first. They arced gently up, their noses reaching toward the sky, and dove back down. As they disappeared below the surface, their tails rose up behind them, dripping water, before sinking slowly beneath the waves.

"They were beautiful," Cooper said. "I've never seen anything like it."

"Every time I see one I feel that way," T.J. said, putting his arm around her.

They stood there, watching as the ripples caused by the whales' diving spread out, mingling with the wake of the boat. Having T.J.'s arm around her felt good, and as Cooper leaned into him she thought, *Maybe there's a point to this dating business after all.*

CHAPTER 10

Annie's bedroom was filled with the smell of the flowers in the garden below her window. There was a gentle breeze stirring the curtains, and they fluttered lazily as the wind carried the scent of lavender and roses into the room. The moon, only a few days past new, was a sliver in the sky outside. In the yard below them Kate saw fireflies flickering softly as they flew among the trees.

"I just love this room," Kate said. "It's the perfect place for working magic."

Annie, who was busily arranging white votive candles into a circle in the middle of the floor, laughed. "Don't forget that the first spells I did here were utter failures," she said.

"That was a long time ago," Kate replied.

"Not all that long," objected Annie. "We've just gotten better at it."

She stood back and admired her handiwork. She was getting a lot better at making the circle look right. In the beginning her circles had always been a little lopsided. But this one was a nice full moon shape, and she nodded approvingly.

"Are you ready to start?" she asked Kate.

Kate nodded. She walked over and picked up the backpack she'd brought with her. "I've got everything in here," she said, placing the bag in the center of the circle of lit candles.

"I almost forgot the cauldron," Annie said, going to her desk and fetching the large iron pot that sat beside it. She'd bought the cauldron as a special present to herself, and she was really pleased with how witchy it looked sitting in the sacred circle. "Are you going to tell me what we're doing with it?"

"Not until we've cast," said Kate.

Annie sighed. Kate had been very mysterious about what kind of ritual she'd come up with for them to do. Annie had asked her numerous questions but she hadn't offered up any information. All she would tell her was that they needed the cauldron.

"Shall we get started, then?" Annie asked.

Kate nodded. The two of them stood side by side at the edge of the circle. They were both wearing white robes, and their feet were bare. Annie raised her hands and began the familiar rite of casting the circle.

"East," she said. "Creature of air. We ask you into our circle to bless us with your gift of creativity."

They turned as Kate spoke the next invocation. "South, creature of fire, we ask you into our circle to bless us with your gift of determination," she said.

There was another turn and then Annie continued with, "West, creature of water, we ask you into our circle to bless us with your gift of change."

Kate finished summoning the directions by facing the north, lifting her hands with the palms out and intoning, "North, creature of earth, we ask you into our circle to bless us with your gift of protection."

"By the powers of earth, water, fire, and air, the circle is cast," the two girls said, stepping into the circle.

"I'd like to invoke one of the goddesses," Kate told Annie, who nodded in assent.

Kate lifted her hands up once more. "Athena," she called out. "Goddess of wisdom and healing. I ask that you join us in this sacred circle and lend to us your gifts of healing." *We need all the help we can get*, she added to herself, hoping that some of the skills Athena was known for would add themselves to the ritual they were about to do.

When she finished she knelt, as did Annie. The cauldron was between them on the floor, and they were surrounded by the flickering light of the candles. Annie watched as Kate opened her backpack and began to remove a series of objects.

"I really wish Cooper was here," Kate said. "It feels weird without her."

It was the first ritual they'd done without their friend. Annie had also been disappointed that Cooper had refused to participate. But she knew that they couldn't let that distract them.

"You can't think about that," she told Kate. "This isn't about her. It's about us and the magic we're going to do. If you think about her you won't be able to focus your intention properly."

"I know," Kate said. "But I still wish she was here."

Annie looked at the things Kate had brought with her. There was a glass jar filled with water, several bags of what looked like herbs, and what looked like a ball of soap.

"What is all of this stuff?" she asked.

Kate held up the jar. "This is water from the ocean," Kate said. "Seawater is supposed to be really good for doing magic. And these are different herbs," she continued, indicating the little bags. "Sage, lavender, milk thistle, vervain, and lemon balm."

"And we're doing what with it?" queried Annie.

Kate unscrewed the top from the jar of seawater and poured it into the cauldron, where it splashed merrily as it filled the vessel about halfway. Then she opened the packet of milk thistle and sprinkled it in. "We're making a bath," she told Annie as she added the lemon balm to the concoction.

Annie helped her put the remaining herbs into the water. Then Kate pushed back her sleeves. "Now help me mix it up," she said.

The two of them put their hands into the water and started stirring. Their fingers touched as they swirled the water around.

"As we mix it up, think about pulling white light

up from the earth and letting it run out through your fingers," Kate instructed.

Annie had used the white light meditation many times, and had no problem imagining the light filling her body and moving out through the ends of her fingers and into the water. She pictured the cauldron filling with the light, and watched as it swirled around in bright circles.

"The idea is to turn the cauldron into a healing bath," Kate said. "All of these herbs are supposed to promote healing in the body. I looked them up in one of the books I've been reading."

After a few minutes of stirring, Kate took her hands from the water and picked up the ball of soap.

"Now what?" asked Annie. "We wash our hands with that?"

Kate shook her head. "This represents Aunt Netty's cancer," she said. "We're going to bathe it in the water. As we do, we imagine the cancer getting smaller and smaller, just like the soap will."

"I get it," Annie said. "Sympathetic magic. Sort of like the time you put a spell on that doll that looked like Scott."

"I thought we weren't going to dwell on anything negative," Kate said, giving Annie a withering look.

"Sorry," Annie said sheepishly as Kate put the ball into the water.

Kate took a deep breath and began rubbing the soap with her fingers. "Try to picture the cancer shrinking," she said as she passed the soap into Annie's hands.

Annie ran her fingers over the slippery surface of the ball, working the seawater and the herbs into it. She imagined the healing light inside the cauldron surrounding it and eating away at it. As the lather foamed around her hands she imagined the cancer becoming smaller and smaller.

"This feels really powerful," she said to Kate. "It's like we're working the magic right into Netty's bones."

Kate took the soap from her and moved it around in the cauldron. Like Annie, she pictured her aunt's cancer floating in a cauldron of warm water and herbs. She tried not to be sickened by the thought. Instead, she lovingly caressed the soap as she worked it down to a smaller and smaller ball.

She had no idea if what she was doing would work. She'd gotten the idea out of a book, but that spell had suggested imagining the soap ball as a problem that was bothering you. It had been Kate's idea to make the soap represent the cancer. It had seemed like a good idea. She hoped it was.

As she moved her hands over the soap she tried to imagine Athena there with them, adding her hands to the cauldron. She frequently had trouble picturing the different goddesses in her mind, but this time she saw almost immediately a pair of hands joining with hers and Annie's. She felt the healing touch of them, the warmth that flowed from the fingers as they helped her wear the soap cancer down.

In her mind she looked up to see Athena's face, and she was startled to see that the image that came to mind was that of Cooper. She looked at Kate with a mixture of sadness and strength. Then the face changed and it was no longer Cooper's. It was a face Kate had never seen before, a strong, noble face framed by black curls.

Kate passed the soap ball back to Annie and let her work on it for a while. She tried to picture her aunt in the hospital, getting better. She imagined the doctor coming to tell them that the cancer was gone and that Aunt Netty could go home whenever she felt like it. She saw her mother's face break into a smile of relief and joy, and she pictured them all hugging one another. It all felt incredibly real, and she was sure that the spell was working.

The two of them worked on the soap ball for almost an hour, passing it back and forth and bathing it in the herbal water. Gradually it wore down, first to the size of a golf ball, then to the size of a gumball, and finally to the size of a pea. Then, while Kate was working with it, the last few bits fell apart and dissolved into the now-foamy water.

"Now what do we do with it?" Annie asked Kate.

"I'm going to put it back in the bottle and return it to the sea," Kate said. "That way it mixes with the ocean and is dispersed back into nature."

Annie helped her pour the water from the cauldron into the jar. Kate put the lid back on and set it aside.

"That felt really good," she told Annie. For the first time since hearing her aunt's diagnosis she felt a sense of hope. The ritual had gone well, and she was encouraged by the feeling of peace that had come over her.

"It felt good to me, too," Annie agreed. "How do you think it will work?"

"I'm not worried about that," Kate said. "I think we just have to wait and see." But inside she was imagining Dr. Pedersen calling her house to tell them that Aunt Netty's cancer had magically disappeared. Everything about what they'd done seemed just right, and she knew that the magic would do its thing and start working right away.

"Do you want me to come with you to the ocean?" Annie asked.

Kate shook her head. "I'd like to do that on my own, if you don't mind," she said. "Is that okay?"

"Sure," answered Annie. "I think my part is done anyway."

They opened the circle by thanking each of the directions for coming. Kate gave an extra thanks to Athena. Then they extinguished the candles, gathered everything up, and put the room back to its normal state.

Kate changed back into her street clothes and shouldered her backpack. "I'm going to go finish this up and call it a night," she said.

Annie hugged her friend. "I hope it all works," she said.

Kate smiled. "We gave it everything we had," she said. "Now we just have to sit back and let it do its thing. I'll let you know as soon as I hear anything."

Kate went downstairs. Annie's aunt was making coffee in the kitchen, and Kate waved to her as she passed through.

"Brewing up magic potions again?" Sarah Crandall asked with a smile. She knew that the girls were involved in Wicca, and she didn't mind their using the house for their rituals.

"I hope so," Kate said, feeling against her back the weight of the jar of water that was weighing down her pack. "Good night."

She left Annie's house and walked through the warm night to the bus stop. She didn't have to wait long, and soon she was passing through town on her way to the beach.

I always seem to end up back here, she thought as the bus came to a stop and she got off. The beach had played a large role in many of the important moments in her life: her breakup with Scott, her first kiss with Tyler, and the first real ritual she had done with Annie and Cooper. It was special to her. And now she was there again, this time for perhaps the most important reason.

She walked down the long flight of wooden

steps to the beach. Because it was so nice out, there were a number of people sharing the expanse of sand with her. Most were just walking along enjoying the weather and the waves splashing on their feet. Others had brought their dogs to romp in the surf, while some were sitting on the rocks, alone or with partners, looking at the waves.

Kate walked past all of them to the far end of the beach. There a line of large boulders separated the main area from a small cove. This was where she and her friends sometimes performed rituals. It was also where Kate went when she wanted to be by herself. Most people didn't know about the cove, so it was usually deserted.

That was the case now. As Kate stepped carefully over the rocks, she saw that no one else had taken up residence in the area. She was relieved. She'd half expected to find a group of kids having a cookout, or someone else who liked to think of the cove as a private place enjoying the solitude.

But she didn't have to worry about that. The little beach was all hers. She sat on one of the rocks, removed her shoes, and rolled her pants up as far as she could. Then she took the jar of seawater, herbs, and soap out of the backpack and held it in her hands as she walked to the edge of the water.

Even though it was very warm out, the water was cool. Kate was always surprised at how cold the ocean was, even in summer. There was a shock as the first wave crashed over her feet. But she quickly adjusted to it, and then the coolness felt good. She loved how a little bit of the sand washed away with each new wave, and how her toes dug in as she waded farther out.

She walked until she was standing up to her knees in the ocean. As the waves came in they swirled around her legs, tickling her. She stood there with her eyes closed, feeling the swell and the pull of the tides. She imagined the whole ocean, so vast and deep and mysterious, and herself standing on just the very edge of it. It made her feel so small and insignificant, but at the same time it made her feel as if she were connected to a great cycle of nature that had repeated itself endlessly, without change, for millions of years. The water in the jar she held had come from that same ocean, and now she was returning it so that it could become part of the sea once more.

She removed the lid from the jar and held it up to the little piece of moon that peeked out from behind the passing clouds. Tipping it, she listened as the water containing the pieces of the soap ball trickled into the waves. As it did she found herself singing one of the chants they often sang at rituals.

"We all come from the Goddess," she warbled in her off-key voice. "And to her we shall return, like a drop of rain flowing to the ocean."

She hadn't intended to sing the song. It had just come to her, a memory she'd forgotten about until that moment. But now it seemed absolutely perfect.

Like the rest of the ritual, it had simply appeared when she needed it.

When all of the water had been emptied from the jar, she immersed the jar itself in the waves and let them wash it clean. Then she stood for a few more minutes, enjoying being part of the sea, before wading out and sitting once more on the rock to let her legs dry.

Beyond the rocks she could hear laughter. *When Aunt Netty is better I'll bring her here and we'll laugh like that*, she told herself. The spell was going to work. She just knew it. As she put on her socks, she recalled the face of Athena and how reassuring her look had been.

Then she remembered that first it had been Cooper's face she'd seen. What did that mean? She had no idea. Probably it was just a leftover thought from earlier in the evening. She pushed the thought to the back of her mind. It was time to get home. Tomorrow she would go to the hospital to see Aunt Netty, and maybe she would tell her all about the beach and how the cove was waiting for her.

CHAPTER II

Annie stepped back and looked at the wall. The paint was drying a shade lighter than it had gone on, and she liked the effect. It reminded her of the sky on a clear summer day.

"What do you think, Mr. Rowe?" she asked.

Ben Rowe turned around and stared at the wall. There was blue paint on his glasses and on the overalls he'd put on. "I think you should call me Ben," he said. "You're making me feel older than I am."

"I mean about the paint," Annie said. "Do you like the color?"

"Little girl, through these eyes it's a perfect blue."

"Good," Annie said. "Because this wall is just about finished. How are you doing over there?"

"Not so good, I'm afraid," Ben said. "I keep pushing the paint one way with the brush and it keeps running the other direction. I think the brush must be defective."

Annie went over to inspect his work. She'd

assigned him the wall with the window, figuring that it had the least amount of space to cover. Now she was thinking that maybe she'd made a mistake. He'd gotten almost as much paint on the window as he had on the wall, and it had made quite a mess.

"Why don't you take a break," she told the old man. "You can be the foreman for a while."

"I like that plan," Mr. Rowe said. He put his drippy paintbrush in the bucket and went to sit on the tarp-covered chair in the far corner while Annie set to work cleaning up the window.

They'd gotten quite a bit done in the few hours they'd been working. Two whole walls and part of a third were nearly completed, and once she cleaned up the window and evened out Ben's spotty job, they would be done. A few places might need a second coat, but already the room had taken on a much improved air.

"This sure beats how I usually spend my Sunday mornings," Ben told her as she worked. "Generally, I'd be sitting in there with the rest of them old buzzards while some do-gooder tried to get us to sing hymns."

Annie chuckled. Now that she wasn't afraid of him anymore, Ben's cantankerous demeanor made her laugh. She loved to imagine him terrorizing the nurses and the other volunteers who came to Shady Hills and had the misfortune of getting in his way. In only a few days he had become her personal project, and she was pleased at the headway she was making. She'd even convinced him to let her repaint his dreary old room, although he'd insisted it be blue.

"You shouldn't be so hard on the staff," she admonished Ben.

"Why not?" he snapped. "I've got to have some fun, haven't I? I'm an old man. I'm supposed to be cranky."

"I think maybe you overdo the cranky old man bit sometimes," Annie told him.

"You've got a smart mouth for someone who was only born yesterday," Ben said.

Annie laughed again, making the brush slip so that she smeared the window and had to wipe it clean again.

"Maybe we should take a break and let this dry," she said. "Then we can come back and finish up later."

"And what do you propose we do in the meantime?" Ben asked her. "Hold a barn dance?"

"I've got that covered," Annie said. She disappeared into the hallway and came back carrying a picnic basket. "I brought lunch."

"You mean I have to miss the gruel and bread crusts they usually give us for Sunday dinner?" he said.

"I know it's a hardship," replied Annie. "I thought we could take it into the garden and eat there."

"Suit yourself," answered Ben, standing up.

Annie went into the tiny bathroom attached to his room and washed her hands. When she came back out Ben was wearing an old hat.

"I've got to keep myself out of the sun," he explained when he saw her eyeing the ratty-looking hat. "You don't want me to get heatstroke, do you?"

"Heaven forbid," said Annie dramatically.

The two of them walked down the hall to the exit, which Annie pushed open to let the old man through. They went into the large garden that surrounded the back of Shady Hills. Annie had seen it all through the windows of the rooms as she cleaned them, but she hadn't yet stepped foot in it. Now she looked around at the plants and trees.

"This is gorgeous," she commented. "You should come out here more often."

"I'm allergic to fresh air," Ben grumbled as they walked along.

Annie groaned. "Do you like *anything*?" she asked him.

"I like the smell of whatever's in that basket," the old man answered.

"That's roast beef sandwiches and apple pie," Annie told him. "I made the pie myself."

"I hope it's good," he said. "I'm a stickler when it comes to pie."

"I'm sure you'll hate it," Annie told him.

She found a big old tree and spread out the blanket she'd brought. Then she helped Ben sit down, and she laid out the contents of the picnic basket for his perusal. He lifted the various containers, opening them up to see what was inside. Several times he sniffed them and made faces Annie couldn't read.

She dished out the food and handed Ben his plate. He poked at it with his fork and took a tiny bite of everything. Then he looked at Annie. "It's good," he said.

"You sound surprised," she said.

He shrugged. "I wasn't sure how it would be," he said. "It's been a long time since I've had home cooking."

"Well, you'll have it more often now," she said. She'd already spoken to Mrs. Abercrombie about having Ben come to her house the following week for Sunday dinner. She wasn't going to tell him about it until later in the week, though, because she wanted it to be a surprise.

They ate in silence for some time, each of them chewing happily. Once again Annie congratulated herself on taking a third chance on the old man. She'd been so close to giving up on him, and she was thrilled that she hadn't. Spending time with him had been a real experience, and he seemed to be enjoying it as much as she was. While he was still his usual brusque self, he had mellowed a bit, at least with her.

When Ben had finished his lunch Annie reached in and brought out a big piece of apple pie. As she handed it to him she said, "Even if you don't like it, pretend you do. I worked all morning on that. I even made the crust from scratch."

He cut off a big bite and popped it into his mouth. He chewed slowly and swallowed. "Is there cinnamon in there?" he asked. "And clove?"

Annie nodded. "The clove wasn't in the recipe, but I thought it would be a nice addition. Is it too much?"

"Just right," Ben said, taking another bite. "Just like I'd make it myself if I still could. Clove was always my secret ingredient."

"You baked?" Annie said, astonished.

"I had to do something after the war," Ben told her. "There's not much call for soldiers once the fighting's over. I was a baker. Worked in some of the finest restaurants in this country."

Annie was speechless. She hadn't really thought about Ben's life before coming to Shady Hills. She knew about his brother, but that was it. Now she found herself wondering what else she didn't know about him.

"Tell me about baking," Annie said.

Ben rubbed his chin. "It's like magic," he said after a minute or two, and Annie noticed that his voice had taken on a different quality, softer and almost dreamy, as if he were telling a story to a group of children. "I liked pies the best, the way the fruit filled up the pan and how the crust went over the top like a blanket. I only used the freshest fruit," he continued. "Peaches in August, berries in the fall.

Blueberries as soon as they were ripe enough. I got the recipes from my grandmother—kept them in a little book. I think she must have got them from *her* grandmother, they were so old. She's the one who taught me how to make crust the right way. None of this store-bought stuff they have now."

The old man's face had relaxed, and for a moment Annie could see in it the reflection of the face in the photograph. *He was handsome once*, she thought.

"Everybody loved my pies," Ben said assertively, giving Annie a firm look. "Said they were the best they'd ever tasted."

"I'm sure they were," she said. "And I'm glad I didn't know you were a baker before I made this one. I never would have given it to you."

"You could use a little help," he said. "But it's not bad. Not for a beginner."

Annie figured that the paint should be ready for a second coat, but she wasn't ready to go inside yet. Now that she'd found out a little bit about Ben's life, she had other questions. She wasn't sure how much he would tell her, though, so she chose her words carefully.

"Did you have any other family besides Tad?" she asked gingerly, afraid of spoiling the nice time they were having by being too personal.

He shook his head. "We had a sister, Rachel, who died when she was six. Scarlet fever. But that was the whole family. My father died not long after the war, and my mother several years after that."

"And you never wanted to get married?" Annie said. It was the question she'd really wanted to ask him all afternoon, but she'd been afraid to because it seemed too personal.

Ben sighed. "No, I never married," he said simply. Annie thought that he was through answering the question, but a minute later he resumed speaking. "I wanted to," he said. "I was in love with a girl. Violet Marshall. I met her one summer while I was working at a seaside resort in northern California. She was also working at the hotel, as an assistant manager. She had the most lovely dark eyes, and the sweetest voice."

"So why didn't you?" asked Annie. "Didn't she love you?"

The old man fixed her with a look. "Is it that hard to believe that a young lady would fall in love with me?" he asked.

"I didn't mean it that way," Annie said.

"Yes, she loved me," Ben said. "We were very much in love. But we didn't marry. At the end of the summer I went away without telling her why."

"That's terrible," said Annie. "It must have broken her heart."

"Yes," said Ben. "It probably did. I know it broke mine."

"Then why did you do it?" Annie exclaimed. She hated the idea that Ben had been in love and lost it for some reason.

He sighed. "I didn't want to lose her," he said. "I didn't want to wake up one day and find her gone, the way Tad was. I was afraid of being too much in love with her."

Annie didn't know what to say. It was the most open, honest thing he had told her yet. And worst of all, she knew exactly what he meant.

"You didn't want to get hurt," she said. "You didn't want to let her get too close because then it might end and you'd be alone again."

She was speaking slowly. She'd thought that Ben was the one telling his story, but suddenly she realized that it was her story, too. It was the same way she'd felt since the deaths of her parents. She'd been afraid to let people get too close, or to get too close to them, because they might leave her.

"It was a mistake," the old man said. "I was wrong. I thought that I could escape by choosing to be alone. But all I did was shut myself away. I didn't avoid the pain by pretending to choose solitude for myself. I only made it worse."

He looked at Annie. His eyes were sad, but at the same time she could see in them a glint of happiness. What was he thinking about? she wondered. Was it Violet?

"You're the first friend I've had in many years," he said to her, and she knew then what he was thinking about. It was her.

She couldn't speak, not because she was afraid of bursting into tears but because she didn't need to say anything. The look in Ben's eyes told her everything she needed to know, and she knew that saying anything in response would only spoil the moment.

"Don't run away from people, Annie," he said softly, his tough exterior dropping completely for a moment. "Don't be afraid to love them."

Annie didn't know if Ben really understood how close to home he'd hit. Was he speaking about himself, or did he see in her eyes that she, too, was terrified of losing the people in her life? It didn't matter. She understood what he was saying to her, and she knew that their friendship had changed both of their lives forever.

"What do you say we get back to painting?" Ben said, suddenly sounding like his old self again. "I can't sit out here all day yakking about the past."

Annie nodded, clearing her head. She was still thinking about his last words to her as she gathered up the dishes and put them back into the picnic basket. Then she helped Ben get to his feet again, and the two of them walked back to the home.

"I don't know what I'm going to do now that I have this grand new room," Ben said as they went inside. "I feel like the shabbiest thing in there."

"Maybe we'll have to do a makeover on you," Annie teased. "I'll set my friend Kate loose on you. She'll have you in something from J. Crew in no time."

"Are all your friends as sassy as you are?" he asked.

"Worse," said Annie, thinking about Cooper's sharp tongue. "Much worse."

"I don't think I want to meet them, then," said the old man. "One of you has been hard enough to get used to."

They returned to his room and spent the next hour finishing up the paint job. When it was finished, Annie looked around. The room looked a thousand times better than it had before. Even the worn furniture had taken on a look of new hope now that the walls weren't so dingy.

"When the curtains are back up this will be perfect," Annie said.

Ben was sitting in his chair, his eyes closed.

"Have I worn you out?" Annie asked him.

"I'm seventy-eight years old," he replied. "And I've just eaten more at lunch than I usually eat in a week. I think I need a nap."

"I'll leave you alone, then," Annie said. "We're done here anyway."

She moved his bed back so that it was close to the wall but not touching it. Then she made sure that his window was open so that the paint could dry and the fumes wouldn't bother him.

"You're all set," she said. "Want me to tuck you in?"

"There you go again," said Ben, sitting wearily on the edge of his bed. "Getting smart with an old man. You should be ashamed of yourself."

"I think you can handle it," said Annie. She

kissed him on the cheek. "I'll see you tomorrow."

"Don't let Abercrombie see you doing that," Ben chided her. "She'll think we're having a torrid affair."

Annie rolled her eyes, waved at him, and left. As she walked through the hall to the front door, she thought again of what he had said outside. What would his life have been like if he'd stayed and married Violet? Would he be at Shady Hills now, or would he be somewhere else, surrounded by people who loved him? What exactly had he given up by leaving her at the end of that summer so many years ago?

And what about her? How many friendships had she passed up because she'd been afraid of getting close to someone? How many opportunities had slipped through her hands because of that fear? The deaths of her parents had taken a lot away from her, but she had let them destroy more than was necessary.

Not anymore, she thought determinedly. She'd been right—Ben Rowe had come into her life for a reason. He was part of her path after all. And now that he was there, she was going to change. She was going to take chances. She wasn't going to lock herself away because it made her feel more secure. She was going to let the world in. She'd already started doing that with Kate and Cooper, and it had completely changed her life. Now she saw that there was even more that she could do.

She exited the building and walked into the glorious afternoon sun, her head filled with all kinds of ideas. But mostly she was thinking about what kind of pie to make for Ben when he came to dinner the next week.

CHAPTER 12

Kate was walking too close to the edge of the cliff. Cooper could see her following the path and walking happily as if she were strolling through a meadow instead of teetering on the brink of danger. She didn't seem to be at all aware of the fact that one wrong move would send her plunging headlong into the abyss that lay at the bottom of the mountain.

"Kate!" Cooper called out as loudly as she could. "Watch out!"

Kate didn't turn around. She kept walking, ignoring Cooper's warning. There was a bundle tied to a stick balanced on her shoulder, and it bounced with each step. Cooper thought that was strange. Then she noticed that Kate was also dressed oddly. She was wearing a funny hat that had three long points sticking out from it.

She's dressed like the Fool from the Tarot deck, Cooper realized. *What's going on?*

She was dreaming. Part of her mind understood that. But it seemed so real. She was standing on a mountain, watching her friend as she traveled a narrow path through treacherous rocks. Cooper knew that it was her job to help Kate, but she didn't know how. She kept calling out her name, but it was as if Kate were deaf. *Or you're invisible*, she thought. Was that it? Was Kate unable to see or hear her?

She ran forward, tugging on Kate's sleeve. Kate paused for a moment, looking around confusedly, and then kept walking as if nothing had happened.

"Kate!" Cooper yelled. "I'm right here! Turn around. You're going to get hurt!"

Again Kate paused for a moment, and again she continued on her journey through the mountains, oblivious to the fact that Cooper was following along behind her.

"Please, Kate," Cooper cried. "Just listen to me."

Kate turned around, looking right through Cooper as if she didn't exist. She shifted the pack on her shoulder, and as she did her foot slipped. She lurched sideways, leaning out over the edge of the path. Cooper could see the ground sliding away from beneath her friend's feet.

"No!" she screamed. She lunged forward, grabbing at Kate. But Kate continued to fall, tumbling over the side of the mountain. As she did, her eyes met Cooper's, and she looked confused.

"Why?" she said before disappearing.

Cooper woke up. She knew that it had all been a dream, but she was still frightened. Her forehead was covered with sweat, and she was breathing hard. She hadn't had a dream as real as that one since her encounters with the ghost of Elizabeth Sanger. But what did it mean? Was Kate really in trouble? Was Cooper supposed to help her somehow?

Kate was dressed as the Fool, Cooper remembered. Was that some kind of a sign? If so, what could it mean? She sat up and thought hard, trying to think of any connection between Kate and the Fool. Then she remembered—Kate had drawn the Fool card in class several weeks ago. It represented the path she was traveling as she studied Wicca.

So why am I seeing her? Cooper asked herself. After her intense experience with Elizabeth's ghost, she knew that her dreams were usually clues to something going on in real life. So what was this one about? Obviously it had something to do with Kate. But what? And why was Cooper trying to warn her?

She thought about it for a long time, but nothing came to her. As far as she knew, Kate wasn't in any kind of trouble. If anything it was her aunt who was in a perilous situation. But the dream hadn't been about Kate's aunt. It had been about Kate.

It was about me trying to help her, Cooper thought. *It was about me trying to help her—and failing.*

Maybe that was it. Maybe the dream wasn't really about Kate, at least not directly. Maybe it was about herself. In the dream she had been trying to help Kate as she walked along her path. But ultimately she had caused Kate to fall by calling out to her. She had distracted her friend, and as a result Kate had fallen from the cliff.

That's it, she thought. *You're afraid that if you try to help Kate you'll end up hurting her instead.*

That made sense. After all, Kate had called her asking for help. But she'd said no. And why? Because she was afraid she'd ruin things. She was afraid that if she got involved in anything having to do with witchcraft it would all go wrong, just like it had on Midsummer Eve.

So it had just been a simple nightmare. In a strange way that made her feel a little better. At least she could try to go back to sleep. She closed her eyes and put her head on the pillow.

But all she could see was Kate's face as she fell off the cliff and looked into Cooper's eyes. "Why?" she said again, and the word repeated itself over and over in Cooper's mind.

She sat up again. This time she turned on the light. She wasn't just having a nightmare. There was some other reason for her dream. Someone was trying to tell her something. She sighed. *I thought I was through with this kind of stuff,* she thought tiredly.

The question now was what she was going to do next. She could stay up all night trying to figure it out, but she knew that would just make her tired and irritable. There had to be something else, something that would help her focus and figure out what the dream was telling her.

Suddenly her eyes fell on the little table she'd once used as an altar. Now it held some books she was reading.

Oh, no, she thought as an idea popped into her head. *I'm not going there*.

She looked away from the table, but her gaze was drawn back to it. Could she really do what she was thinking? Could she do it again? She didn't want to. She knew it was just asking for trouble. But something was urging her to do it.

Reluctantly, she got out of bed and went to her closet. Inside she found the box where she'd packed away the things that had once been on her altar. She took the box out and sat on the bed, holding the box on her lap. She very much did not want to open it. She'd even sealed it with packing tape.

With a sigh she pulled on one end of the tape, ripping it off. Then she opened the box and looked inside. There, wrapped in newspaper, was the goddess statue Kate had given her on her birthday. Cooper took it out and gently unwrapped it. She held the image of Pele in her hand and looked at its face.

"Hi," she said. "Remember me?"

She carried Pele to the table. After clearing the books from the top, she set the goddess on top of it. Then she went back to the box, retrieved the candle that was in it, and put that on the tabletop as well. Still not believing that she was doing what she was doing, she found some matches and lit the candle.

Then she sat on the floor, watching the candle burn and staring at the statue of Pele behind it.

She sighed. What was she doing? She felt like an idiot sitting there in front of the table. She couldn't even think of it as an altar. That was too much. It was just a table with a statue and a candle on it. She hadn't even put the cloth on it first.

"This isn't anything permanent or anything," she said quietly, looking at Pele. "I just want to talk to you for a minute."

She placed her hands in her lap and looked down at them. She wasn't sure what she was doing. In the past she had always been able to use meditation to help her sort through her feelings. Many times she had sat like this, talking to Pele or just letting her thoughts settle as she worked on something that was bothering her.

"It's this Kate thing," she said. "I know she wants me to help her. But I can't. I'd just screw everything up. I'm not doing that stuff anymore. This stuff either," she added as she looked at the flickering candle. "But here I am doing it."

It wasn't working. Her mind was racing, and she couldn't focus her thoughts. They kept running one way and then another, like mice being chased around by a cat. She would manage to grab one and then another would dash by, breaking her concentration so that the first thought escaped.

"What do you want me to do?" she asked Pele angrily, as if she expected the goddess to start talking. "You want something, or I wouldn't have had that dream."

The Pele statue continued to stare back at her with empty eyes. She knew it wasn't going to speak to her. The only time she had received a message from the goddess was during a dream. If Pele wanted to tell her something, why hadn't she appeared in the dream? *Maybe it was just a nightmare after all*, she told herself. Maybe she was just being ridiculous and projecting her anxiety about her strained friendship with Kate into her subconscious.

"I knew this was a dumb idea," she said, standing up. She blew out the candle. Then she picked up the statue of Pele and took it back to the box. Wrapping it up, she placed it inside. The candle she left out because the wax was still hot. She would put that away in the morning.

She put the box back in her closet and returned to bed. What had she been thinking? Why did she think she could just put a statue on a table and ask it to give her advice? That was an act of desperation, something to do because she couldn't think of anything else. But why should Pele give her any messages, especially after Cooper had decided not to be involved in Wicca anymore?

Just forget about it, she told herself as she tried to get back to sleep.

It took some time, but she managed to get to sleep again. Much to her relief, she didn't have any further dreams, about Kate or about anything else.

But she slept poorly, and when she opened her eyes and saw that it was morning, she groaned sleepily. Not only did she have to get up, but it was Monday. There was a tour coming that afternoon, and she had to show them around. It wasn't exactly what she felt like doing at the moment.

She forced herself to sit up. Yawning, she stretched her tired muscles and cracked her neck. Then she stood up and shuffled to the door to find her bathrobe before heading to the shower.

As she reached for her robe she paused. Turning her head, she looked at the table where she had placed the statue of Pele the night before. The candle was still sitting there. Only now it was burning again.

I know I blew that out last night, she told herself. She remembered doing it, because she was always afraid that if she didn't something would catch fire. But if she had blown it out, how had it come to be flickering brightly now?

She walked over and stared at the candle. Was it possible that she hadn't really blown it out completely? No. But there it was, burning as if it had been going all night. Quite a bit of wax was gone, so she knew that it must have been burning for at least several hours.

She glanced at the closet, where she knew the Pele statue was sitting in the box. Walking over to it, she pulled the door open and pried the lid of the box off. She took the statue out and carried it back to the table, where she set it beside the candle.

She stood looking at the statue and the candle. What was she doing? She couldn't bring herself to say that she'd set the altar up again. But something was going on, and she needed to figure out what it was. As much as she didn't want to think that she was even thinking about being involved with her old practices, she knew that something had changed during the night.

"I'm going to take a shower," she said out loud. "Try not to burn the place down while I'm gone."

She went into the bathroom, turned on the shower, and stepped inside. The warm water soothed her tired body, and she took her time lathering herself with soap and rinsing off. She poured shampoo into her palm and washed her hair, letting the water stream down her face. As she stood there, the steam rising up around her, she thought about what was happening.

Was Pele really sending her a message telling her that it was time to come back? That seemed implausible. But how else could she explain the candle relighting itself? *Maybe you got up and did it yourself*, she thought.

No, she had to accept that the goddess was telling her something. She just wasn't sure she wanted to hear it. What if Pele was suggesting that Cooper needed to return to Wicca? Was that it? She didn't think she could do that. No, she *knew* she couldn't do that. She'd promised herself that she was done with it.

Yeah, she reminded herself, *just like you said you would never set up the altar again.*

But she hadn't set up the altar. Not really. She'd just put the statue out for a little while, until she figured out what was happening.

That sounds like you're back to me, the voice in her head mocked.

She turned off the water and grabbed a towel from the rack. As she dried herself she thought about what to do next. She had the tour at two. That gave her the whole morning to do something else.

She trotted back to her room, shut the door, and dressed. She pulled on jeans and an old Missing Persons T-shirt she'd found at a used clothing store. She left her hair alone, liking the way it dried naturally into an unruly rat's nest. Then she sat on the edge of her bed and looked at the candle, which was still burning on the table.

Since you've gone this far you might as well keep going, she told herself. She went back to the closet and looked in the box. There was the box of Tarot cards she'd been using in class. She hadn't done a lot with them—Tarot was more Annie's thing than hers—but she had done readings from time to time.

She took the cards with her as she sat in front of the altar again. As she shuffled them she tried to clear her mind. She didn't want to affect the reading by forcing any of her worries onto the cards. It was hard enough for her to remember what everything meant. She didn't want to end up convincing herself of something just because she wanted to believe it.

When the cards were shuffled, she cut the deck into three piles. She selected the middle one and set it on top of the other two. Then she turned over the first three cards. It was the easiest kind of reading she knew how to do.

The first card was the Tower. It showed a tall brick turret. Storm clouds circled the top, and lightning was striking it. A fire burned in one of the windows, and a figure tumbled down through the clouds that surrounded the tower. Cooper knew that the card indicated an unexpected event that was difficult and perhaps painful. But it also suggested that the person would gain important knowledge because of what happened.

"I guess that's supposed to be me," she said out loud. She thought about her ordeal in the woods a few weeks before. "That would definitely qualify as a catastrophe," she said. And it had definitely changed her life. She'd learned that magic couldn't always be controlled, and it had caused her to end her study of Wicca.

She looked at the second card. "The Three of Swords," she mused. It showed a large heart pierced by three wicked-looking swords. It was an ugly card, and it made her feel bad. It represented a relationship that had somehow gone bad. It disturbed her even more because she knew that the relationship in question was the one among herself, Annie, and Kate. The three swords could easily represent them. Looking at the card, she felt a sense of lone-liness creep over her. Had her actions caused this separation? She knew that they had, and she felt ter-rible about that.

She quickly moved on to the last card. It too was from the suit of Swords. But it was the Ace. The sin-gle large sword was surrounded by two roses, one red and one white. The card indicated a power of some kind, a power that could be used for either great good or great destruction.

"So which one is it?" she asked herself.

The reading wasn't very helpful. She knew what all the cards meant. But how did they fit together? Clearly, her relationship with her friends had been disturbed by her behavior. And if her dream was really true, then she was afraid of trying to become involved with what was happening to Kate because she feared what would happen to her. But what was this great force? That's what she didn't know. And what was it going to do?

She was back at square one. She had a lot of clues, but no real answers. All she knew was that she didn't want to get involved but everything was pulling her in that direction anyway. She could keep running, or she could keep taking little steps for-ward and see what happened.

She looked up at the statue of Pele. "Okay," she said as she put the Tarot cards back in their box. "Just remember—you started it this time."

CHAPTER 13

On Tuesday morning Kate was more anxious than usual to get to the hospital. Aunt Netty had been undergoing treatment for almost a week, and surely they would be able to judge how well she was responding to it. There was also the matter of the ritual Kate and Annie had done on Saturday night. Kate had been watching her aunt carefully for any signs that she might be improving. Although it had only been two days, yesterday Aunt Netty had been hungry, and her nausea from the chemicals being used to attack her cancer had suddenly gone away. Everyone had been surprised to find her happily eating her supper and even asking for more, but Kate had secretly jumped for joy. Her spell seemed to be doing exactly what she'd hoped it would do.

When her mother pulled the car into the hospital parking lot, Kate practically ran to the front doors. She went inside and hit the up button for the elevator, pacing impatiently as her mother caught up with her.

"What's the rush?" she asked.

"I just want to see if Dr. Pedersen has any news," Kate responded.

"She's not even due to come up until ten," Mrs. Morgan reminded her daughter. "You've got fifteen minutes."

Kate continued to pace. Why was the elevator taking so long? She watched as the numbers lit up, going lower as the elevator descended to the lobby. Finally the doors opened and she hopped on, pressing the button for the third floor.

"Kate, I don't want you to get your hopes up," her mother said. "I know you want there to be good news. But it hasn't been that long, and there might not be any change."

"I know," Kate said. "But I have a good feeling about this." She wished she could tell her mother that she'd done a ritual to help Aunt Netty. But she couldn't. Not yet. *Maybe if everything works out right I will*, she thought. That would be a good way to bring up the subject with her family. They'd be so happy that Aunt Netty was better that they'd be more open to hearing about Wicca and what it could do.

The doors opened, and Kate stepped out with her mother. She looked down the hall to her aunt's room and saw that the door was open.

"She's awake," Kate said, hurrying down the hall and waving to the nurses as she passed their station. They all knew her by sight now and waved back.

Kate found her aunt sitting up in bed, poking at

a plate of scrambled eggs and toast. When she saw her niece, Netty smiled.

"Come on in," she said. "I was just trying to decide what kind of animal these eggs came from. I think they were laid by a pterodactyl."

Kate kissed her aunt and then sat on the end of her bed. "How are you feeling?" she asked.

"Great," Aunt Netty said. "Well, relatively great. Anything is better than throwing up every half hour. But really, I feel a lot better. It's like something's changed. I don't know what, but I just feel different."

It's magic! Kate wanted to shout. *It's the magic!* But she just smiled and grabbed her aunt's hand. "I'm so happy," she said.

Mrs. Morgan walked in and greeted her sister. "Has the doctor been by yet?" she asked.

"Not yet," said Netty. "I'm expecting her any minute."

"Aunt Netty just told me that she feels a lot better," Kate told her mother.

"I'm glad to hear it," her mother responded.

Kate looked around the room. "You know what would make this place even better?" she said. "Flowers. I think I'll go get some."

Before anyone could reply she ran out of the room and down the hall. There was a florist in the hospital lobby, and she wanted to pick up some beautiful flowers to celebrate the good news that Aunt Netty was feeling better. As she rode down, she thought about how nice it would be when her aunt could come home and they could get back to having fun like they did before she got sick.

In the flower shop, she looked at everything. She considered roses, but then put them back and chose a big bunch of gerbera daisies. They were pink and yellow and orange, and they reminded Kate of the flowers from a Dr. Seuss book. She knew Aunt Netty would love them because they were unusual.

When she returned to the third floor she saw that her aunt's door was closed. *Dr. Pedersen must be in there*, she thought excitedly. She went to the door and knocked. A moment later her mother opened it.

"I'm back," Kate said as she entered the room. "Do you have something I can put these in?"

When no one answered her she looked around and saw that nobody was smiling. Her aunt was looking out the window, and Dr. Pedersen was standing awkwardly beside the bed.

"What's wrong?" she asked.

Her mother put her hand on Kate's shoulder. "Dr. Pedersen was just going over Netty's test results," she said quietly. "There's no improvement."

"But what about the treatments?" Kate asked frantically. "Didn't they work?"

"They appear to be working," the doctor told her. "But they're taking quite a toll on your aunt's body."

"So what happens now?" asked Kate. "Do we

just sit here and let the cancer take over her whole body?"

"Kate," her mother said. "Try to calm down."

"No!" Kate shouted. She was starting to shake. "This isn't what was supposed to happen! She was supposed to get better. The cancer was supposed to go away."

She was upset about the doctor's news, both because it meant that her aunt was still sick but also because it meant that her ritual had failed. How could it? Everything had gone so well. It had felt so right. What had happened?

"I understand your frustration, Kate," Dr. Pedersen said. "But you have to understand that when it comes to cancer there's no one way things are 'supposed' to happen. We try what we can and we hope for the best, but sometimes the body has a mind of its own."

Kate stared at her. What was she saying, that Aunt Netty *wanted* to be sick? That she was somehow responsible for the disease inside her? She found herself wanting to defend her aunt, to tell the doctor that she had it all wrong. Aunt Netty didn't want to be sick. Nobody would want to be sick.

"What *do* we do now?" Mrs. Morgan asked.

Dr. Pedersen sighed. "We wait some more," she said. "We continue with the treatment to try to knock out the cancer that's invaded Netty's system before it attacks anything else. If we can get it to slow down or stop altogether, I think she stands a pretty good chance of recovering."

"And if you can't?" Aunt Netty asked quietly. "Then what?"

The doctor looked at the three of them. "Then the cancer attacks more of your organs and your body shuts down," she said.

Kate heard her mother draw in her breath sharply. She knew that the doctor's words were a shock to her and that she was trying to stay calm. She saw Netty close her eyes and lean her head back. What was she thinking? Was she thinking about how she might die?

"I wish I had better news than that, but I don't," Dr. Pedersen continued. "But please believe me when I say that we're doing everything we can."

"I know you are," Aunt Netty said, trying to smile. "And believe me, I appreciate it."

The doctor left the room, and Kate stood, holding the flowers, while her mother and aunt looked anywhere but at each other. Kate was angry. She could feel it boiling inside of her, sitting in the pit of her stomach like a hot coal and radiating out to fill her with misery and rage. Why was this happening? And why was it happening to Aunt Netty, who had never done anything bad to anyone in her entire life? It just wasn't fair.

She needed to get out of there. She couldn't stand looking at her aunt for another minute knowing that she was dying and that the one thing Kate had tried to do to help her hadn't worked.

She needed to get away.

"I have to go," she said, putting the flowers down on the chair beside her.

"Kate," her aunt said. "It's okay."

"No, it isn't," Kate said, beginning to cry. "It's not okay at all."

Her mother tried to stop her as she left, putting her hand on Kate's arm. But Kate shook it off. "I have to go," she said again. "I'll be home later."

She knew that running out wasn't the right thing to do. She knew that her mother and her aunt were shocked at her behavior. But they didn't know how much she had believed that the spell would work. They didn't know how sure she'd been that the energy she'd put into it would surround Aunt Netty and make her well. They didn't know how much it hurt her that she'd failed.

She didn't even wait for the elevator, taking the steps two at a time as she ran down the stairs and out of the hospital. She was walking fast, not knowing where she was going but needing to be away from that room where the sickness was overwhelming. She had to keep walking, keep moving so that she wouldn't cry or scream or hit something, the way she wanted to.

She kept walking through town, not really paying attention to where she was going. Then she realized that she was walking toward the water. She almost turned around, heading for the bus and home, when she had an idea. She could go to Crones' Circle. She hadn't been there very much lately, and maybe Tyler would be there helping out for the day, as he sometimes did. She could talk to him.

She hurried in the direction of the store. When she arrived she pushed open the door and scanned the room for Tyler's familiar face. But all she saw was Simeon, the gray cat who lived in the shop. He was sleeping in a patch of sun by the big front window, his paws curled over his face.

"How can you look so happy?" she said accusingly, and Simeon opened one big green eye and blinked at her.

"Kate," said Sophia, coming out from the back room. "Nice to see you."

"Is Tyler around?" Kate asked.

Sophia shook her head. "Not today," she said. "I think he's doing some work for Thatcher. They're building cabinets over at Thea's house."

Kate nodded. Tyler had been spending a lot of time with Thatcher, one of the members of the Coven of the Green Wood. Thatcher had been a master carpenter for years, and he was teaching Tyler how to work with wood.

"Are you okay?" Sophia asked. "You look a little upset."

"It's my aunt," Kate said. "She's not doing very well."

"I'm sorry to hear that," said Sophia.

Kate felt herself beginning to cry again. "I don't

understand it," she said. "I did a ritual to help her, and it didn't work."

Sophia put down the books she was unpacking. "You did a ritual?" she asked.

Kate nodded.

"Tell me about it," Sophia said.

Kate sniffled, holding back the tears. She told Sophia about the soap ball, and the ritual, and about putting the water back into the sea. Sophia listened attentively.

"Did your aunt know you were doing the ritual?" she asked when Kate had finished.

Kate shook her head. "You know I can't talk to my family about Wicca," she said, more defensively than she meant to.

"I know," Sophia remarked. "But do you remember what we talked about in class, about doing magic for other people against their will?"

"But this wasn't against her will!" Kate protested. "It was to help her."

Sophia smiled. "I know that," she said. "And your ritual sounds beautiful and very thoughtful. But you still did it not knowing if it's what your aunt would want or not."

"Why wouldn't she want it?" Kate asked, confused. "Why wouldn't she want to get better?"

"I didn't say she doesn't want to get better," Sophia said. "But in order for magic like that to work properly, the person you're doing it for has to help out as well."

"What do you mean?" asked Kate. "You mean she has to be there in the circle with me?"

"Not necessarily," Sophia answered. "What I mean is that she has to want you to do the ritual for her. Whether or not she physically participates doesn't really matter, although it helps. What really matters is whether or not she's open to the process. You can want to do something for someone, but if that person doesn't want you to then all of your effort will be wasted."

"So if I had told her that I was doing it she'd be better?" asked Kate. "Great. That makes me feel even worse. Next thing you'll be telling me is that all of the energy I sent out bounced back as negative energy and will cause her cancer to spread."

"I can assure you that *that* is not the case," Sophia said. "If the cancer spreads it's because it's cancer, not because you did anything wrong. And to answer your other question, no, your aunt wouldn't automatically get better just because she knew you were doing the ritual. Healing magic is like any other magic. It works when the conditions are right. You can't just heal someone because you want to heal her. That would be like trying to manipulate things to work out so that you're happy. Well, maybe that's not how things are supposed to work out."

"You mean maybe Aunt Netty is supposed to die?" Kate asked incredulously.

"That's putting it too simply," Sophia said.

"What I mean is that your aunt's body is going through changes for some reason. When you did healing magic for her, you tried to alter the course of those changes. That's not a bad thing. But there may be reasons her body needs to go through this. In that case, you're trying to stop something that, for whatever reason, needs to occur."

"I don't see how not wanting her to die could be a bad thing," Kate replied.

"It's not a bad thing," Sophia told her. "That's what I'm trying to tell you. But trying to heal her because *you* want her healed isn't the best way to go about it."

Kate thought about what the other woman was saying. "I think I get it," she said after a moment. "It's like when I tried to make Scott fall in love with me. He might have done it anyway, but when I tried to force it to happen I caused a lot of problems."

"Right," said Sophia. "Although in this case I don't think you caused any problems. I think you just expected too much."

"So if it's possible to do healing magic that works, isn't there *something* I could do for Aunt Netty?" Kate asked.

Sophia looked thoughtful. "Yes," she said. "There is. But it's risky."

"I don't care," Kate said. "Whatever it is, I'll do it."

"We have a lot of talented healers in our group," Sophia continued. "We've often done healing rituals for people, either in our various covens or in the community."

"You mean we could do a group ritual?" Kate asked.

Sophia nodded. "It might help. As you know, the more people you have working on a spell the more powerful it can be."

"So why is that risky?" Kate asked. "It sounds great to me."

"You're forgetting what I said earlier," Sophia responded. "You need to ask your aunt if it's what *she* wants."

All of a sudden Kate understood what Sophia was saying. If she wanted to help Aunt Netty, she had to tell her about her involvement in witchcraft.

CHAPTER 14

"You're sure slow today," Annie commented as she walked with Ben down the hallway of Shady Hills toward the physical therapy room. "Didn't you get enough sleep last night?"

"I'm old," Ben groused. "I sleep a lot. I'm like a bear. I need a good ten hours or I don't feel right."

"In that case you must not have had a good night's sleep since about 1958," teased Annie.

Ben humphed at her, but she knew he wasn't angry. He enjoyed her company. In fact, she'd pretty much been assigned to him ever since the staff learned that she had made friends with the old man. They were all perfectly happy to pawn him off on her, as all of them had had more than their share of run-ins with Ben since he'd come to the nursing home.

When they entered the physical therapy room, the aide looked up. "Well, well, well," he said brightly. "It's Mr. Rowe. How are you this morning?"

"Old!" Ben bellowed. "How do you think I am?"

"Well, let's see if we can't get you feeling

better," the young man said.

"I didn't say I felt bad," Mr. Rowe said. "I just said I was old. And you'd better not pull on my knee the way you did last time. I couldn't walk for two days after you manhandled me."

Annie giggled to herself. She knew Ben was putting on a show for her. The fact was that Karl, the physical therapist, was actually a really nice guy. Ben went to him three times a week because of his bad knee, which caused him a lot of pain.

"I'll be gentle with you," Karl said as Ben sat down.

"I'll come back for you in an hour," Annie said to her friend. She leaned down and added in a whisper, "Try not to scare him, okay?"

Ben waved her away, but he smiled as he did it. Annie left him there and went back to changing the sheets on the beds. She was enjoying it more now that she'd been there for a while. Besides Ben, she had made friends with a lot of the residents, and now they talked to her as she pushed the laundry cart up and down the halls.

"Hi, Annie," said Mrs. Pennington in room 312.

"Hi," Annie said back. "How's your bird today?"

"Oh, fine," the old woman answered. "Listen to him sing."

Annie paused outside her door, listening to the chirping coming from inside. Mrs. Pennington had a blue parakeet that she kept in a cage, and it was her pride and joy.

"Ulysses is really going at it today," she told Annie. "I think he must like you. He starts up whenever he hears the cart coming."

"He probably just thinks it's dinner coming," Annie joked as she continued on her way.

Shady Hills was becoming a very special place to her. She knew a lot of the people by name, and she had started to learn their stories. She had discovered that a lot of the old people had led really interesting lives and that they loved it when someone asked them about themselves. She spent most of her free time talking to one person or another, hearing about what they had done when they were younger and finding out all kinds of fascinating things.

Mr. Torrance in room 167, for example, had once been an actor in silent films. Miss Grace in 233 had been one of the first women news reporters on the radio. The more questions she asked, the more Annie realized that the residents of Shady Hills weren't just people who had been thrown away or who had slipped between the cracks. They were people with thoughts and ideas and memories, and all they wanted was someone to talk to them. For one reason or another they had ended up there, usually because they had no family who could take care of them. But each of them was like a book waiting to be opened and enjoyed, and Annie was enjoying reading each of them.

Ben, of course, was her favorite. She loved the time she spent with him, and of all the residents she felt the closest to him. Since their talk on Sunday he hadn't said anything else about Violet or about his past, but talking about it had changed many things for Annie, and she appreciated his talking to her that way.

She thought about how quickly her life had changed as she stripped the sheets from a bed and put new ones on. In just over a week she had completely changed her view of Shady Hills. She didn't even notice the smell anymore. To her it had become just another part of the place, just like the green tiles in the hallway, the squeaky wheel on the laundry cart, and Mrs. Abercrombie's clipboard. She was glad she had volunteered there, and she was looking forward to being there for as long as she could.

Suddenly her thoughts were interrupted by a commotion in the hallway. She went to the door of the room she was in and looked out. Several nurses, including Mrs. Abercrombie, were scuttling down the corridor. They had anxious expressions on their faces, and they seemed to be in a terrible hurry.

"What's going on?" Annie asked one of the nurses as she passed by.

"A guest has collapsed," she said.

Annie left the laundry cart and followed the nurse, thinking that she might be able to help if they needed an extra pair of hands. As they passed the doors of the rooms she saw some of the residents peering out, looking concerned.

"Who is it?" one of the old women asked Annie.

"I don't know," she said. "But I'm sure it will be fine."

She rounded the corner behind the nurse and stopped dead. The nurses were all running into the physical therapy room. After a long horrible moment of not being able to move, Annie ran after them.

When she stepped inside she saw someone lying on the floor. Karl was bent over the figure, and several of the nurses were also on the ground. People were calling out, and their mingled voices added to the confusion. But although she didn't know what was going on, Annie was sure of one thing—it was Ben they were talking about.

"What happened?" Mrs. Abercrombie asked Karl.

"He collapsed," Karl told her. "He was walking on the treadmill over there, and he just crumpled."

"Someone call 911," another of the nurses said.

"We already have," answered someone else. "They're on their way."

Annie was paralyzed with fear. She wanted to step closer and see if Ben was breathing, but she didn't dare. Besides, she didn't want to get in the way. Karl was bending over Ben's face, and it looked like he was performing CPR on him.

There was a clattering in the hallway, and a man in uniform burst through the door. "Clear the room," he cried out as Annie realized that he was an EMT.

Two other technicians followed behind him, carrying medical kits. Annie and the nurses left the room, and the last technician in shut the door behind her, closing them out. The nurses, however, remained clustered around the door, looking at one another.

"Is he going to be all right?" Annie asked, finally finding her voice.

"They'll do everything they can for him," one of the nurses assured her.

"But what's wrong with him?" Annie asked.

Mrs. Abercrombie came and put her arm around Annie's shoulder. "We won't know for a while," she said. "I know this sounds impossible, but it would be best if you went back to work. It will help calm the other guests."

Annie nodded. Feeling dazed, she walked back to the room she had left when she'd heard the noise. The bed was still half finished, and numbly she took up the sheet and tucked it in. She didn't even think about what she was doing, she just did it. When she was done she moved on to the next room.

"Who was it, dear?" asked a woman in a wheelchair who passed the door on her way somewhere else.

"Ben Rowe," Annie informed her.

The woman sighed.

"But I'm sure he'll be okay," Annie added quickly, not wanting her to get the wrong idea. After all, the EMTs were still doing their jobs.

The woman gave Annie a little smile and

wheeled off. Annie turned to her work and concentrated on making the bed. It was easier than worrying about Ben. That was up to someone else now. All she could do was wait.

She finished one floor and started on the next. Room after room went by without word from Mrs. Abercrombie. *What can they be doing to him?* Annie wondered as she dumped dirty sheets into the hamper and picked up yet another set of clean ones. It had been almost an hour since the technicians had arrived. Surely if something was terribly wrong they would have taken Ben away by now. She reassured herself by thinking that probably he had just been overtired and fainted.

She entered the next room. When she looked, she was surprised to see that it was Ben's. She hadn't even thought about what floor she was on or where she was. But there she was, standing in the middle of his room with the freshly painted walls, the cheerful curtains, and the new bedspread she'd picked out for him just the day before.

She went to the bed and stripped it. Then, very carefully, she remade it using new sheets. She wanted her friend to have somewhere nice to sleep when he came back upstairs. She hoped that he wouldn't have to go to the hospital and that soon he could be resting comfortably in his own bed. Maybe she could even read to him and tell him how he'd given her a scare. *He'd probably like knowing that he frightened me*, she thought as she folded the top sheet over and pulled the comforter up over it.

On her way out she stopped and picked up the framed photo on the dresser. She looked at Ben and Tad, smiling, and she felt better. Ben looked happy in the picture. Even though she knew he missed his brother terribly, it made her feel good to think that maybe she had filled a little tiny place in Ben's heart that had been left empty by his brother's death. She knew that he had helped her erase a little bit of the pain caused by losing her parents, and she hoped she had done the same for him.

She went back into the hall, where she saw Mrs. Abercrombie walking toward her. She waited until the other woman reached her before asking, "How is he?"

The nurse looked at her kindly. "I'm afraid he died, Annie."

Annie felt as if she'd been slapped. The hallway lurched, and she gripped the side of the laundry cart frantically. She felt Mrs. Abercrombie steady her, and she leaned against the wall to steady herself.

"How?" she said, unable to get any other words out.

The nurse sighed. "He had a heart attack," she said.

Suddenly, Annie thought about how tired Ben had looked over the past few days. Why hadn't she said anything to the nurses?

"He hadn't been feeling well," she told Mrs. Abercrombie, even though it was too late.

"He had a heart condition," the nurse informed her. "He was on medication for it. Apparently, it finally was just too much for him."

"It was the treadmill," said Annie angrily. "He shouldn't have been on it."

Mrs. Abercrombie shook her head. "That was just coincidental," she said. "If it hadn't been that it would have been something else. Ben's heart just wasn't working right anymore."

Annie looked into the nurse's face and knew that she was telling the truth. The woman's eyes were sad and kind, and it was too much for Annie to take. She started crying, loudly and fiercely.

"It's not fair," she said. "He was finally starting to enjoy himself. He was going to come to my house this Sunday for dinner."

She felt like a baby, crying and saying whatever came into her mind. But she couldn't stop. There was a horrible pain tearing through her, and she needed to let it out. When Mrs. Abercrombie hugged her, she began to wail.

"He can't be gone," she said as the nurse stroked her hair and told her it would be okay. "He just can't be."

Suddenly she was six years old again. She was standing in the garden of her family's house in San Francisco while flames came out of the windows and a neighbor held her and told her that everything would be okay. But things hadn't been okay. Her parents had died. And things weren't okay now because Ben was dead and the friendship they'd been building was suddenly over before it could even really begin. It was happening all over again, and she couldn't take it.

She slumped to the floor, the nurse holding her as her body collapsed. She leaned against the wall and let the tears come. They ran down her face and fell onto her shirt, and she did nothing to wipe them away. She needed to cry. She needed to grieve. Thinking about Ben, gone, was too much.

"I didn't even get to say good-bye to him," she said to Mrs. Abercrombie, but really speaking to herself. "I didn't get enough time with him. I didn't get to tell him how much I liked being his friend."

"I think he knew," the nurse said, crouching down and wiping Annie's face with a handkerchief. "I think he knew exactly how you felt about him."

But Annie wouldn't be comforted. Her hurt was too new, too fresh. She needed to cry much more, and she did. The nurse let her sit there while she shook and sobbed, sometimes rubbing her eyes but mostly just letting the tears fall where they may. She didn't care how she looked or who saw her. She missed her friend. She missed him more than she had missed anything or anyone in a long time. She felt as if a wonderful new present she'd been given had been snatched away from her before she'd had a chance to enjoy it properly.

"You should probably go home for the day," Mrs. Abercrombie said after Annie had been crying for ten minutes. "Would you like me to drive you?"

Annie nodded. "Thank you," she said. The idea of having to ride the bus was too horrifying, not because she was afraid people would think badly of her but because she knew that if she saw anyone who reminded her of Ben she would start crying all over again.

The nurse helped her up and walked with her back to the office, where Annie grabbed her things. Mrs. Abercrombie told another nurse to take over for her, and she walked Annie out. In order to get to the front door they had to pass the physical therapy room, and Annie was relieved that the door had been shut again.

"Is he in there?" she asked as they passed it.

Mrs. Abercrombie shook her head. "The EMTs took him to the hospital in the ambulance," she said.

Annie nodded. *At least someone is taking care of him*, she thought as they left the building. She wished it could be her, but she was glad that Ben was at least off the floor and being looked after.

Mrs. Abercrombie drove her home, with Annie giving her directions in a tired voice. She was worn out from sobbing so much, and she was exhausted from unhappiness. It still all seemed like a terrible dream, and she kept hoping she would wake up and find herself in bed with the alarm ringing and her aunt calling her to breakfast.

"I've seen a lot of guests die in all the years I've

been in this business," Mrs. Abercrombie said as they sat waiting at a light. "It never gets easier."

Annie didn't say anything. She couldn't explain to the nurse just what Ben Rowe had meant to her, what he still meant to her, even though she had known him for only a few days. He hadn't been just a patient, or just another bed whose sheets needed changing. He'd been someone she'd been looking forward to knowing for a long time. But now he was gone, just like that, and she couldn't get him back. All those chances she'd thought she'd had to know him better were gone in an instant.

"I know this won't help right now," the nurse said. "But try to think of Ben the way he was when you saw him at his happiest. That's the way he would want you to remember him. Then again," she added, "since it's Ben Rowe we're talking about, maybe he'd prefer it if you remembered him at his crankiest moment."

Annie laughed in spite of her sadness. She looked over at Mrs. Abercrombie.

"It would be hard to pick just one," she said.

When they reached Annie's house, Mrs. Abercrombie said, "Take the day off tomorrow. I'll call you to let you know about funeral arrangements."

"I didn't think there would be one," Annie said, surprised. "He didn't have any family, did he?"

The nurse shook her head. "No, but all the guests receive services as part of their stay with us."

Annie nodded. "Thanks," she said. "For everything."

Mrs. Abercrombie drove away, and Annie let herself into the house. Her aunt and Meg were gone, but there was a note for her on the kitchen counter.

> *Annie:*
> *Kate called. Said she had big news.*
> *We'll be back around 6:00 for dinner.*
> *AS (and Meg)*

Annie put the note in her pocket and went upstairs to call Kate. Whatever Kate's news was, she hoped it was better than hers.

CHAPTER 15

T.J. was playing when Cooper arrived at his house. He was listening to a tape they'd made of a song they were working on, and he was playing his bass line along with her guitar. His long fingers moved up and down the neck of his bass quickly and confidently, and Cooper stood in the doorway watching him for a few minutes before he even noticed she was there.

"It sounds good," she said when he looked up, saw her, and turned off the tape.

"Not bad," he agreed.

That was one of the things Cooper liked best about him—he knew when what he played worked and when it didn't. There was no false modesty with T.J., and there was no empty boasting. When they played, it all came together because they both knew that it was about the music and not about them.

Cooper unpacked her guitar, plugged into the amp that sat across from T.J.'s in the empty garage, and started playing around. T.J. listened for a minute and then joined in. They played like that for a while, each of them trying different things, and then T.J. stopped and looked at her.

"You're not really into it," he said. "What's up?"

Cooper picked a few more notes, then let her guitar hang against her chest. "Is it that obvious?" she asked.

T.J. nodded. "I think you started playing the new Britney Spears single," he said. "That means bad news."

Cooper gave him a half smile. "It's nothing major," she told him.

T.J. nodded. "Uh-huh. Should I be worried here? Is this where you tell me it's been fun but we make better friends?"

Cooper laughed. "No," she said. "Is that really what you thought?"

T.J. shrugged. "You never know," he said. "So if it's not me, or us, then what is it?"

"Do you have to know everything?" asked Cooper.

"I think it's sort of traditional to care about the person you're going out with," answered T.J. "But if you don't want to talk, that's okay. We can just play, as long as you cool it with the teen queen pop music stuff."

"No," said Cooper. "It's okay. We can talk about it."

She was surprised that she wanted to tell T.J.

what was going on. But she trusted him. And ever since Kate's call that afternoon she'd wished she had someone to discuss it with. But it was going to take a lot of explaining, and part of her was apprehensive about telling T.J. too much.

"You remember all the stuff with the dead girl, right?" she said. "Elizabeth Sanger."

T.J. nodded. "How could I forget?" he asked.

When the newspaper had printed a story about Cooper and her visions of Elizabeth Sanger, Cooper had feared that it would end her friendship with T.J. and the other band members. But T.J. had been really cool about it, and he had never brought it up again. Cooper had always appreciated that, because she knew he must have wondered what it was all about. Now she was going to tell him.

"Well, that was all true," she said. "I did see her ghost."

T.J. raised an eyebrow but didn't say anything.

"There was a lot of weird stuff that happened around that time," Cooper continued. "Kate and Annie were all mixed up in it, too."

"They see dead people, too?" asked T.J.

Cooper shook her head. "Just me," she told him. "But we're all in this group together, and it all kind of goes together."

"A group like Scooby and the gang, or something else?" T.J. asked. "I'm not following you."

Cooper sighed. "It's going to sound a little weird," she said. "So just listen. Kate, Annie, and I were in this group that studies Wicca. You know what that is, right?"

"I saw *The Blair Witch Project*," T.J. answered.

"It's not like that at all," said Cooper. "This is a group that studies *real* witchcraft, as in the religion. It's run by these cool people who own a bookstore in town. Anyway, we were going to this group and—"

"You keep saying you *were* going," T.J. interrupted.

"Right," said Cooper. "I don't go anymore."

"But Kate and Annie do?" T.J. said.

Cooper nodded. "It's just me who's opted out."

T.J. was looking at her with an expression that made it clear he was wondering why she wasn't still in the group.

"We'll get to why I'm not in it anymore later," Cooper said. "The point is that the three of us were in this group. We also did stuff together—rituals and things. Is this getting too freaky?"

"Not so far," T.J. replied. "I'm still a little fuzzy on what it's all about, but I think I get it. You guys were witches."

"No," Cooper said. "Just studying it. We, I mean they, Annie and Kate, don't have to decide if they want to do the full-blown witch thing until the year and a day of study are over."

"Which is when?" asked T.J.

"April," Cooper said. "After the Spring Equinox. But that's not the point either. The point is that Kate and Annie are still going to the class and I'm not.

That's made things a little sketchy between us. And now it's gotten even sketchier. I told you about Kate's aunt having cancer. Well, they want to do this healing ritual for her, and they want me to help."

"Help how?" T.J. asked her.

"Lend my energy," Cooper said, unable to think of a better way to describe it to him. "Kate and Annie already did one ritual themselves, and I said I wouldn't do it with them. Now Kate wants to do one with some other members of the group. She called today and asked me if I would do it with them."

She stopped her narrative, looking at T.J. for any sign of what he was thinking about all of this. But he just looked back at her with the same open expression he usually wore.

"I really thought I was done with all of this," Cooper continued. "But then I had this dream the other night. It was about Kate, and she needed me to help her and I didn't because I was afraid. And then today Kate told me that she had a vision where Athena had my face. Then there's the whole thing with the candle. Am I making any sense here?"

"Up until those last couple of sentences you were," he said. "You lost me on the vision-Athena-candle part."

"But the rest of it?" Cooper said.

"Mostly clear," he said. "Let me see if I have it straight. You were part of this group that studied witchcraft. Then you dropped out for some reason you'll explain to me later. But your friends are still involved in it, and they're going to do this ritual that they want you to help out with. Only you don't want to."

"Right," Cooper said, relieved that somehow her disjointed story had all come out in the end.

"Why?"

"Why what?" asked Cooper.

"Why don't you want to help them?" T.J. elaborated.

Cooper frowned. "That's the hard part," she told him. "I kind of had a bad experience. With magic. It wasn't fun. Actually, it was really scary. That's why I stopped."

"Before that happened, did you like it?"

Cooper shrugged. "Yeah," she said. "I did."

"And this thing that happened, did it have anything to do with the group?"

"No," Cooper answered. "Not really. It was more of a free-form bad magic kind of thing."

T.J. didn't say anything for a while. He stood across the room from her, silently fingering his bass.

"What?" Cooper said finally, unable to stand the silence.

"I was just thinking about it all," T.J. said. "Kate and Annie are still your friends, right?"

"For the moment," Cooper said.

"And they want you to help them?"

Cooper nodded.

"But you're afraid to because of this thing that happened?"

"That's pretty much it," said Cooper. "What do you think?"

"I think you're a coward," T.J. said.

Cooper stared at him. "What did you say?" she asked, not sure she'd heard him correctly.

"I said I think you're a coward," he repeated.

"How can you say that?" Cooper said indignantly. "You don't even know half the stuff that happened and—"

"How long have I known you?" T.J. asked, interrupting her.

"I don't know," Cooper stammered. "Almost two years, I guess."

"Right," said T.J. "And in all that time I have never once seen you back down from a challenge."

"I'm not backing down!" Cooper said.

T.J. folded his hands across his chest. "Then what are you doing?"

"I'm being careful!" Cooper said. "This stuff isn't a game, T.J. People can get hurt. I almost got hurt."

"But you didn't," he said. "So what are you really upset about?"

She glared at him, fuming. Who did he think he was, anyway? Here she was trying to be the good girlfriend and ask him for his opinion and he had the nerve to . . . to . . . *To give it to you*, a voice in her head said.

"So?" T.J. asked. "What is it you're afraid of?"

Cooper started to say something and stopped. She opened her mouth, trying to think of some smart retort. But she couldn't come up with one. The fact was, T.J. was right. She *was* afraid. But no one had made her say it, and she'd been hiding behind her usual shield of bravado and self-righteousness.

"I'm afraid it won't work," she said finally. "I'm afraid that I'll get into it again and it will all spin out of control like it did before."

"If someone told you that it wouldn't, would you do it?" he asked.

Cooper thought about that. For a while Wicca had been the best thing in her life. Doing rituals with Annie and Kate. Attending events with the members of the coven. Even the first frightening encounters with Elizabeth Sanger's ghost. They had all changed her life in dramatic and wonderful ways.

"Yes," she said. "I would."

"Then like I said, you're being a coward."

"But no one can promise me it won't go bad again," Cooper countered.

"No one can promise you that *anything* won't go bad," said T.J. "No one can tell you that your music will be good, or that you'll always be able to write lyrics, or that you and I will always be together. But you took chances on those things. Are you going to give up on them now because one day they might not work out the way you expect them to, or the way you want them to?

Because if you are, then I don't see much point in us making music or in us being a couple."

Cooper didn't respond. She just stood there, staring at T.J. and thinking about what he'd said. It made sense. There were no guarantees in life. She had turned her back on something because it hadn't worked the way she wanted it to, because for a couple of hours one night she hadn't been in control and that made her angry. It wasn't the magic she was afraid of; it was of not being one hundred percent in control of everything that happened to her. But that was stupid. She didn't need to give up something that had been important to her just because her pride was wounded.

"I hate it when you're right," she said.

"And that's why I like it even more," replied T.J., grinning at her.

"You know, if I'd known this going-out thing was going to mean you get to lecture me, I would never have signed up," Cooper commented.

"You can always back out," he said. "I mean, if you want to be a coward and all that."

"Nah," Cooper replied. "I think I kind of like having a guy who stands up to me when I'm being an idiot."

They spent a couple of hours playing. Now that Cooper had made up her mind about what to do, she found that everything was a lot more fun. The weight she'd been feeling had been lifted, and she saw for the first time just how much she had really missed the idea of practicing Wicca with Annie and Kate. She just hadn't let herself admit that until T.J. had forced her to.

When they were done, she packed up and told T.J. she would call him later on. "I've got something I need to do first," she said, giving him a kiss and leaving him in the garage.

She drove home, parked the car, and went inside to her room. Taking a deep breath, she picked up the phone and dialed Kate's number. As the phone rang and she waited for someone to answer, she looked at the statue of Pele sitting on the table.

"I suppose you knew all along this would happen," she said.

Someone picked up the phone at Kate's house. It was Kate's father.

"Hi, Mr. Morgan," Cooper said. "Is Kate around?"

"Kate?" he yelled. "Phone for you. It's Cooper."

There was a pause as Kate came to the phone. Then Cooper heard her say, "I've got it in my room, Dad. You can hang up."

The second phone clicked as Mr. Morgan replaced it in the cradle.

"Hey," Cooper said, suddenly unsure of what to say.

"What's up?" Kate asked, not sounding particularly excited to hear from her.

"I've been doing some thinking," Cooper began. "Actually, I've been doing a lot of talking. To T.J."

"T.J.?" Kate said.

"Yeah," Cooper said. "We're kind of going out."

"What?" Kate exclaimed, suddenly sounding more like her old self. "*You* have a boyfriend?"

"Well, yeah," admitted Cooper. "But I didn't call you to talk about that. I wanted to apologize."

"You don't have to," Kate said. "I understand how you feel."

"I didn't understand how I felt," said Cooper. "That was the problem. I was all freaked out about what happened up in the woods. But it wasn't about the magic. It was about me. Me not being in control. That's why I bailed. I didn't like not being in charge, you know?"

"That sort of makes sense," Kate told her. "And T.J. helped you realize all of this?"

"Amazing, huh?" Cooper answered. "And you thought Tyler was the only cool guy left. Anyway, I want to talk to you about the ritual."

"What about it?" Kate asked hesitantly.

"Can I still help?" asked Cooper.

Kate paused. "Are you just back for this, or for everything?" she asked.

"I haven't quite decided," Cooper admitted. "I think one step at a time is the best way to go."

"And you're doing all of this because of T.J.?" said Kate.

"Not just him," Cooper told her. "I had a dream about you, too. I didn't say anything before because I still wasn't convinced it meant anything."

"What kind of dream?" Kate said.

Cooper told her about the nightmare she'd had. When she was done Kate said, "You and your dreams. But if it made you think twice about giving up on us, I'm glad you had it, even if you did let me plummet to my death."

"Sorry about that," Cooper apologized. "So, do you still want me?"

"More than ever," said Kate. "We've missed you. Besides, I think we're going to need all the help we can get on this one."

"Have you told your parents yet?" asked Cooper.

"That's next on my list," said Kate. "I think I'd rather tell them that I'm pregnant."

"Just tell me what you need," Cooper said.

"I'm not even sure they'll go for it," said Kate. "So right now just think nice thoughts about them not going through the roof when I bring it up."

"Good luck," said Cooper. "Give me a call when you know what's going on."

"I will," said Kate. "And Cooper?"

"Yeah?"

"Welcome back."

CHAPTER 16

Kate sat on the couch, trying to figure out the best way to say what she had to say. She held her hands in her lap, the right one clutching the left one tightly so that she wouldn't rub them together nervously. She wanted to appear as calm as she possibly could.

Her parents sat across from her, waiting for her to speak. She'd asked them to sit and talk to her for a minute, and she knew they were wondering what she had to say. Kyle was there, too, leaning against the doorway to the living room. While normally Kate would be thrilled that he'd decided not to go back to his summer job for at least another week, she sort of wished he wasn't there.

"I want to talk to you about Aunt Netty," she began. "I have an idea for something that might help her," she said.

"Kate—" her mother said.

"Just listen," Kate interrupted. "I know I'm not a doctor or anything, but just hear me out. Something

Dr. Pedersen said to me the other day got me thinking. She said that sometimes patients who aren't responding well to medical treatment can do better if they have some more spiritual help."

"Spiritual help?" Kyle said, sounding confused. "What do you mean?"

Kate sighed. It wasn't going the way she'd hoped. She was having a hard time explaining to her family what she was talking about.

"She said that sometimes people respond to things like prayer," Kate tried.

Her mother nodded. "We're all praying for Netty," she said. "You know that. Father Mahoney includes her in the prayers every week."

"I know," said Kate. "But this is something else. I was thinking of doing a kind of ritual."

She stopped, waiting for a reaction from her family. But they just stared at her blankly.

"What do you mean, a ritual?" asked her father. "Like in church?"

"No," Kate said. "We could do it right in her hospital room."

"Honey, I'm afraid I just don't understand," said her mother.

Kate shifted anxiously. This was the part she'd been really afraid of. "I know these people," she said. "Sometimes they do rituals to help people get well."

"What kind of people?" her father inquired.

"They're sort of New Agey," Kate said. She couldn't bring herself to say the word *Wiccan* in front of her parents and her brother. She knew that would just frighten them off.

"New Agey?" her mother said skeptically. "How do you know them?"

"Does this have anything to do with that time your friend Cooper got mixed up in that kookiness about ghosts and some girl?" her father asked, sounding irritated.

Kate nodded. "They were the ones who helped her then," Kate said.

Her father groaned. "Those kind of people are just nuts, Katie," he said. "What kind of junk has Cooper been telling you?"

"It's not junk, Daddy!" Kate said angrily. "They're nice people. They're good people. Why can't you just listen to me for a minute?"

"We are listening, sweetie," said her mother gently. "But you're really not making a lot of sense."

Kate calmed herself. "These people do rituals," she tried again. "They help people heal themselves. It's not weird or kooky or anything like that. They just use positive energy to encourage the person's body to get better."

"Sounds like a lot of nonsense to me," commented Kyle. "Cooper listens to these people? I thought she was smarter than that."

"How do you know so much about what they do?" her father asked pointedly. "Have you been to one of these whatever you call them—rituals?"

Kate didn't know what to say. Should she lie to

her parents and tell them she didn't know anything about Sophia, Archer, and the rest of her friends? She knew they would believe her if she did. But that would be like betraying Cooper, Annie, and everything they were working for.

"No," she said, feeling terrible even as she said it. "I've never been. But Annie has, and she said they're really great."

She knew as soon as she said it that she'd made a mistake. Her parents exchanged a look, and then her father said, "So Annie and Cooper go to these things with these people?"

"You're making it sound like something dangerous!" Kate protested. "You don't even know these people. They're really nice. And they want to help Aunt Netty."

"I don't think Netty needs that kind of help," her father said. He started to stand up, signaling that as far as he was concerned the conversation was over.

"Well, Netty wants them to help," Kate said.

Her father sat down again. "You mean you told her this garbage?" he said. He sounded angry.

Kate nodded. "She said it's all right with her. She'd like all of you to be there, but if you won't come she's doing it anyway."

Her mother groaned. "Kate, how could you do this?" she said. "Netty's scared. She's looking for answers. Of course she'd say yes."

"She's willing to try it," Kate said, maintaining her composure. "If she is, why can't you?"

"Because it's ridiculous," said her father. "That's why. I don't know what these weirdos have been telling you, or why someone with your intelligence would fall for it, but I'm telling you it's crap."

"How would you know?" Kate shot back. She'd never yelled at her father in her life, but now she was furious at him. He was passing judgment on people he didn't even know, and on things he'd never even experienced.

"I've had enough of this," he said, glaring at her. "This conversation is over."

He stood up again, but before he could leave the room Kate's mother reached up and took his hand.

"Wait a minute, Joe," she said.

Kate's father paused, waiting for her to continue. Mrs. Morgan was silent for a moment, then looked at her daughter.

"I can't pretend to understand everything you're talking about, Kate," she said. "But I've never heard you be so passionate about something. If you think this will help, and if Netty has agreed to it, I'm willing to give it a try."

"Teresa—" Kate's father said.

"Joe, this is my baby sister we're talking about," Mrs. Morgan said softly. "She's probably dying. Whatever the doctors are doing isn't working, at least not right now. Netty is in pain. I think you know what it feels like to see someone you love hurting."

Mr. Morgan glanced at Kyle, and Kate could see

he was thinking about the time her brother had been injured. When he looked back again, the anger that had filled his eyes had changed to a look of compassion.

"I don't know who these people are that Kate is talking about," Kate's mother continued. "I'm not sure I approve of these rituals her friends are going to. But I'm willing to give them a chance if she says they're okay."

"They are," Kate said. "They're really nice. I've met some of them. And they wouldn't do anything that would hurt Aunt Netty."

"What do we have to do?" asked her mother.

"Just come to the hospital tonight at seven," Kate said. "You don't have to do anything but be there."

Her parents looked at her for what seemed like hours. Then her mother nodded. "Okay," she said. "We'll be there."

"But if this gets weird—and I mean even a little weird—those people are out of there," her father said.

Kate left her family in the living room and went up to her bedroom to call Sophia to tell her that the ritual was on. When she was done she looked up and saw her father standing in the doorway.

"I'm sorry I gave you such a hard time down there," he said.

"And I'm sorry I yelled," Kate replied.

"You're sure these people are on the up-and-up?" he asked.

"Yes, Daddy," Kate said.

He sighed. "And you're sure there's nothing else you want to tell me?"

Kate looked at him. He was looking back at her with an expression of concern. She knew he was worried that she was mixed up in something he wouldn't like. And the truth was that he probably *wouldn't* like knowing that she was involved in Wicca. But it wasn't something bad. She just didn't know how to make him see that. Not yet.

"No," she said. "There's nothing else I want to tell you."

"We'll leave about six-thirty, then," he said before turning and going back down the stairs.

When they arrived at the hospital, Kate saw Sophia and the others waiting in the lobby. She'd asked them not to go up before she arrived, in case Aunt Netty was nervous. When Sophia saw them come in, she walked over, smiling.

"Hello," she said. "You must be Mr. and Mrs. Morgan. I'm Sophia. This is Archer, Thatcher, Robin, and Julia."

The people she'd brought with her all smiled warmly at the Morgans. Kate knew all of them from class, and she had asked each of them personally to come. She'd also asked them to dress in normal street clothes so that her parents wouldn't see them in robes or ritual gear and be freaked out. And she had, with more than a little disappointment, asked

Tyler not to come. She didn't want to have to explain to her parents how he was involved in the group.

"Hello," Mr. Morgan said, somewhat stiffly, as he shook hands all around. "I'm Joe. This is my wife, Teresa, and our son, Kyle. I guess you've already met my daughter."

Kate was spared trying to decide what to say next by the arrival of Annie. She came hurrying in the doors, and she had Cooper with her.

"Sorry we're a little late," she said. "The bus took forever."

Cooper stood back from the group, but Kate went over and gave her a big hug. "You have to save me from my family," she whispered in her friend's ear.

Cooper squeezed her hand. "I think we can handle them," she said.

"Shall we go upstairs?" Sophia asked, picking up the bag she had with her.

"Follow me," said Kate, leading them all to the elevators.

They had to go up in two groups. Kate went first with Sophia and the other members of the coven, leaving Annie and Cooper with her family to take the other elevator.

"How did it go?" Sophia asked her as they ascended to the third floor.

"It was rough," Kate admitted. "I still haven't said the W-word to them yet. Thanks for keeping it low-key."

"No problem," Sophia said as they exited the elevator. "Magic works whether you're wearing a robe or not."

The other elevator opened, and Kate's family emerged with Cooper and Annie. The whole group walked down the hallway to Aunt Netty's room.

"Ready for us?" Kate asked, poking her head in.

Netty was sitting up in bed. She looked pale and tired, with dark circles under her eyes. But she smiled at her niece and waved her in. "Bring it on," she said.

Everyone crowded into the room, and Kate shut the door. She saw that her mother, father, and brother were standing to one side while her friends clustered around the bed. Sophia noticed it as well and turned to the Morgans.

"What we're going to do tonight is really very simple," she told them. "We're going to try to create an atmosphere of calm. Then we'll gather around Netty and form a circle of healing—a ring of light, if you will. We'd like you to be part of the circle, but you don't have to if you're not comfortable with it."

"What is this supposed to do?" asked Kate's father.

"We're going to raise energy," Sophia explained. "We believe that by focusing positive energy around Netty we can encourage her body to speed up the healing process."

She then turned to Netty. "I don't want to give the impression that we're trying to cure you," she said. "You might not even experience anything at all. All we're doing is providing your body with energy it can use if it wants to."

"Kate explained it to me earlier," Netty said. "To be honest, I don't know what to expect. I've never done anything like this."

"Can this make her worse?" Kate's mother asked suddenly.

Sophia turned to her. "No," she said. "Her body is going to do what it needs to do and what it's supposed to do. We hope that will mean healing itself. It might not, but if that's the case it will have nothing to do with what we're doing tonight."

Mrs. Morgan nodded. Sophia opened the bag she'd brought and took out some tall white candles in jars. Kate saw that the others had brought some as well, and now they placed them around the room and lit them. Thatcher turned off the bright fluorescent light, and the room was filled with gentle, warm light, turning it into a cocoon of softly shifting colors.

"Let's gather around the bed," Sophia said, motioning for everyone to form a circle.

They pulled Netty's bed away from the wall so that they could stand all around her. Thatcher, Archer, Julia, Sophia, and Robin took their places, and Annie, Kate, Cooper, Mrs. Morgan, Mr. Morgan, and Kyle stood in the spaces between them. Sophia was at Netty's head, and Thatcher was at her feet. Kate found herself standing with her mother on one side and Archer on the other.

"I'm going to ask you all to close your eyes," Sophia said when they were all arranged.

Kate closed her eyes and listened as Sophia continued.

"Imagine that we are standing in a grove of trees," she said. "We're not in a hospital room. We're surrounded by trees that reach up to a bright, clear sky. The wind is blowing gently and the sun is shining on us. Netty isn't in a hospital bed. She's standing in the center of our circle."

Kate let this image fill her mind. She pictured a lovely grove filled with sunlight. She saw her friends and her family there, and she saw Aunt Netty in the midst of them, smiling and happy. The picture made her smile.

"Now imagine that you have roots going down from your feet into the earth," Sophia told them. "They stretch through the rich soil and continue down until they reach pools of beautiful white light. They enter the light, and now you can draw that energy up through the roots and into yourself. Do that now. Draw that energy up into your body, letting it fill you like a cup."

Kate knew what Sophia was doing. She was casting a circle. But she was doing it in such a way that Kate's family, who had no experience with such things, wouldn't know that's what they were doing.

"Once you feel yourself filled with light, I want you to reach out and take the hands of the people beside you," Sophia instructed them.

Archer took Kate's hand in hers and squeezed it gently. A few moments later Kate felt her mother do the same. *I wonder if she's really seeing the light?* Kate wondered.

There was silence for a minute. Then Sophia spoke again. "Now that we are joined, let the light flow from your fingers into the circle. It will join with the light of the people around you and form a circle around Netty."

In her mind, Kate saw the light slip from her fingertips, merging with the light from Archer's fingers and her mother's fingers. She envisioned the light flowing among everyone in the circle, growing stronger and brighter as the circle was made whole.

"Netty, you are surrounded by the circle of our light and love," Sophia said, her voice low and soothing. "In this circle you are safe. Nothing can harm you. Can you feel that?"

"Yes," Netty said, sounding surprised. "I can."

"This light is going to grow," Sophia said. "It's going to fill the circle. The light is for you, Netty. You can dance within it. You can let it warm you. You can let it embrace you. It is the light of those who love you."

Kate's mind was filled with a vision of this circle of light. It was golden in color, and it pulsed with an energy of its own, as if it was a living thing that was moving around and with Netty as she danced inside it. Kate looked at her aunt's face in the vision and saw her smiling and laughing, radiant with the light.

"Take the light into you, Netty," Sophia said. "Let it fill you. As it does, imagine it surrounding the cancer inside you. Imagine it transforming the cancer, not fighting it but embracing it and changing it, turning it into pieces of light that are absorbed into the circle. The rest of you, continue to see the light flowing out of you, washing over Netty."

Kate felt her mother grip her hand more tightly. How was she reacting to the ritual? Did she think it was nonsense, or was she really seeing the same thing Kate was seeing? She wished she could ask her, but she knew that right now she had to hold her concentration.

They stood in the circle for a long time. Kate had no idea exactly how long. Sophia continued to talk throughout the ritual, telling them to see Netty in the light and telling Netty to let the light fill her and carry off the cancer piece by piece. As it went on, Kate found herself growing tired. She knew this was because of all the effort she was putting into the ritual, but she didn't know how long she'd be able to do it.

Then, when she was growing really tired, Sophia brought the ritual to an end.

"Netty, we're going to open the circle now," she said. "But the light won't go away. It will still be within you. You will carry it with you, and it will continue to heal you. When you think about it, remember the love that you've felt here tonight. Remember the love of your sister, your niece, your family and friends. Remember that you always have that love, and that its power is as strong as the sun. And now I want us all to open our eyes."

Kate opened her eyes. The first thing she did was look at her mother, and she saw that her face was damp with tears. She looked around at the others and saw that they were all smiling. Even her father looked peaceful.

"Let go of the hands you're holding," Sophia said. "But know that even though this circle is now open, it is not unbroken. You have created a safe place for Netty with your energy and with your love. It is a place she can return to whenever she needs to."

Kate released Archer's hand. Her mother continued to hold hers for a moment and then she, too, let go. Kate looked at her aunt. Netty was looking back at her with a serene smile on her face. She was almost glowing.

"I don't know what you all did exactly," she said. "But I feel like I could sleep for a week. That was better than all the drugs they've given me to knock me out."

"We'll let you get some rest, then," Sophia told her kindly.

They turned on the light and blew out the candles, returning them to the bags they'd come in. The members of the coven said good night to Netty and filed into the hallway. Kate followed them.

"Thank you so much for doing this," she said to Sophia. "All of you. I really appreciate it."

"It wasn't just us," Sophia said. "It was you, too. And your family."

Kate looked at Cooper and Annie. "I'll call you guys tomorrow, okay?"

Everyone left, and Kate went back into her aunt's room, where her family was gathered around the bed. She felt a little of her apprehension return as she waited to see what they would say.

"They seemed like nice people," her mother said.

"What did you think, Dad?" Kate asked nervously.

"I don't think I was very good at all of that imagining stuff," her father answered. "But it didn't seem too weird or anything."

Kate looked at Kyle. "Who was that cute girl standing next to me?" he asked, grinning. "And do you think she'd want to go out with me?"

CHAPTER 17

Annie stood in the graveyard next to Mrs. Abercrombie. No one else was there. There hadn't been a memorial or anything, and there was no minister to say anything about how much Ben Rowe had been loved and how he was at rest now. It was just Annie, the head nurse, and the fresh dirt that marked where Ben's casket had been buried earlier in the day. A simple headstone listed his name and the dates of his birth and death.

"Do you think he would have wanted some kind of inscription on the stone?" Mrs. Abercrombie asked Annie. "I couldn't think of anything."

"How about 'Go Away'?" Annie said.

The nurse laughed. Despite the fact that they were the only ones there, it wasn't a somber or depressing moment. Annie was glad that there hadn't been some elaborate church service. This way she could say good-bye to her friend in peace, without a lot of people around.

"Are you doing okay?" Mrs. Abercrombie asked her.

Annie nodded. "It still doesn't seem quite real," she said. "I still expect to hear him yelling at someone for something."

"I know what you mean," the nurse said. "Every time I walk by his room I get ready to hear him complaining about something. Then I remember that he isn't there."

It had been three days since Ben's death. Annie hadn't returned to Shady Hills. She didn't want to see the empty room where Ben had lived, the blue walls they'd painted together. She still cried for him whenever she thought about how they were just starting to know one another. But the tears were coming less frequently, and she had started to be able to remember all the good things about having known him.

Doing the ritual for Kate's aunt the night before had helped. She hadn't been sure that she'd be able to do it. The idea of going into a hospital where someone was dying—where lots of people were probably dying—had frightened her. But standing there in the circle, her hands linked with those of Thatcher and Robin, she'd felt herself letting go of some of her sadness and fear. Although the ritual had been for Kate's aunt, she had drawn strength from it as well. She'd seen that the circle didn't have to disappear just because people died or people went away. The love they left behind was still there, and she could experience it whenever she thought about them.

Ben was gone. She couldn't change that. She would never listen to him rant again. But he was still a part of her life, just like her parents were. The gifts he'd given her hadn't disappeared with him, and no one could take them away from her. He'd taught her how to face her fear of making new friends, and he had shared his story with her. While she would give a lot to see him again, she was comforted by knowing that like everything in nature, he had simply moved on.

"So are we going to see you anymore?" Mrs. Abercrombie asked her.

Annie looked at the nurse. "Is Monday okay?" she asked.

Mrs. Abercrombie smiled. "You aren't giving up, then?"

"You won't get rid of me that easily," Annie replied. "Where there's one crabby old person there are sure to be more."

Unexpectedly, the nurse hugged her. "I'm glad you're staying," she said. "You have a good heart. Not many people would have kept trying with old Ben."

Annie didn't know what to say. She had never felt she was doing something brave. In fact, she'd been terrified most of the time. But she knew she had to keep going to Shady Hills. It had changed her life already, and she had a feeling there was more for her to learn there.

The two of them walked back to Mrs. Abercrombie's car and got in. As they drove out of the cemetery Annie looked back at Ben's grave. *I'll come visit you*, she said silently. *I promise.*

"Could you drop me off at the hospital?" Annie asked. "I have to meet a friend there."

The nurse was happy to oblige, and drove Annie to the visitors' entrance. As Annie got out, Mrs. Abercrombie reached into the backseat.

"I almost forgot," she said. "This is for you."

"What is it?" asked Annie, taking the small package and looking at it.

"Some things Ben wanted you to have," the nurse replied. "Oddly enough, he left a note in his dresser saying that if anything happened to him you should get these."

The nurse drove away, leaving Annie standing there looking at the package. She was almost afraid to open it. Tentatively, she looked inside the bag and pulled out two items. One was the picture of Ben and Tad. As she gazed at it she felt herself starting to cry again, so she quickly put it back in the bag and looked at the other thing that was in there.

It was a little book. The cover was faded, and it had been taped together many times. Annie gingerly lifted the cover to see what it was. On the first page was a stained piece of paper, yellowed with age and covered in faded writing.

"Ethel's Blueberry Pie," she read.

It was Ben's recipe book. Annie couldn't

believe it. She turned the pages carefully, looking at each one in wonder. There were recipes for all kinds of pies, cakes, and cookies. Each one had notations in various inks and handwritings, as each subsequent cook had added her or his comments and suggestions like "more sugar" or "use only fresh lemons." Which ones were Ben's? she wondered.

She held the book in her hands. It was such a treasure, and Ben had left it for her. She was overcome with emotion as she thought about what it had meant to him, and now to her. She couldn't wait to take it home and read it from cover to cover. Even more, she couldn't wait to try the recipes.

She walked into the hospital and went to the third floor. She found Kate in her aunt's room, sitting in a chair and watching Netty as she slept.

"Hey," Annie said. "How is everything?"

Kate came into the hallway, shutting the door behind her. "Mom is with the doctor now," Kate said. "They ran some more tests and she's got the results. They didn't want to wake Aunt Netty up, so they're down the hall."

"Have your parents said anything more about the ritual?"

Kate shook her head. "I think they'd rather not know too much," she said. "I suppose that conversation is coming, but not right now. Kyle's been the worst. He has a crush on Robin."

Annie rolled her eyes. Then she noticed Mrs.

Morgan coming down the hall, and she said, "Here comes your mom."

Kate's mother walked up to them.

"Well?" Kate asked.

"There are still spots on the bones," Mrs. Morgan said.

Kate groaned, but her mother held up her hand. "That's not all," she said.

Kate looked at her, waiting for the rest of the bad news.

"The cancer," her mother said, "hasn't spread any farther. Plus, Netty's system seems to be fighting the cancer more efficiently than it has been. Her white blood cell count is down, which means the new treatment has slowed the rate at which the cancerous cells are spreading."

"So it's *good* news?" Kate said, needing reassurance.

"Yes," her mother said. "Dr. Pedersen said it's as if her body decided to wake up and start fighting. There are no guarantees, and she could just as easily start getting worse again, but for now she's doing better."

Kate gave a little hop. "I knew it would help!" she said excitedly.

Her mother looked at her and Annie and didn't say anything. Kate wondered what she was thinking. Did she believe that the ritual had done anything to help Netty? Did she think it was all just coincidence? Kate wanted to ask her, but she knew she wouldn't. For the moment the subject was closed. But that didn't stop Kate from being so happy she could burst.

"Come on," she said, taking her mother's hand. "Let's go tell Aunt Netty the good news."

Later that night, the three friends sat in Annie's room eating pieces of blueberry pie. Annie had taken it out of the oven only half an hour before, and it was still warm and dripping with juice. She had put vanilla ice cream on top, and it had melted over the sides of the pie, mingling with the blueberries.

"This is just about the most amazing thing I've ever had in my mouth," Cooper said, taking a big bite.

"It's like eating summer," Kate added, licking her fork.

"Not bad," Annie said critically. "I think it needs a little lemon juice next time."

They ate silently for a few minutes. Then Kate put down her plate and said, "This has been a wild couple of weeks."

"You're telling me," Cooper agreed. "I got a boyfriend, Annie lost Ben, and you sort of told your parents about being into Wicca."

"I didn't quite tell them that," Kate said. "And by the way, they think you're kind of weird."

"What else is new?" said Cooper.

"It's like we all got our challenges at the same time," commented Annie.

"And we all met them head-on," said Cooper. "Or at least from the side on."

"The point is that we did it," Kate remarked.

"So what happens now?" Annie asked, voicing the question they all were thinking. "Cooper, are you going to come back to the class?"

Cooper nodded, her mouth full of pie. "Ifm pttm trbckup," she said.

"What?" Kate asked.

"I said, I put my altar back up," Cooper repeated more clearly. "Pele and I had a little talk. I don't think we'll have any more problems. And I talked to Sophia and she said I can come back to class."

"What about T.J.?" Annie asked her. "Kate said you told him."

"Yeah," answered Cooper. "We haven't had a real in-depth talk about it, but he seems cool. To tell the truth, I think it turns him on knowing he's kissing a sort-of witch."

"I wish the idea of witchcraft turned my parents on," Kate said. "I'm not looking forward to that little chat."

"Do you guys realize our year and a day is one third over already?" Annie said, counting the months off on her fingers.

"That went fast," said Cooper. "It feels like it was just last week that Kate came running to us asking for help."

"I did not come running," said Kate indignantly.

"Yes, you did," Annie teased.

"Okay," Kate admitted. "Maybe a little. But if it weren't for me and that spell, we wouldn't be sitting here now. So you have me to thank for this pie."

"All hail the witch queen," said Cooper dramatically, pretending to bow to Kate.

"Seriously," Annie said. "We've come a long way. I'm really proud of us."

"Me, too," added Kate after a moment. "We've been through some weird stuff."

"And some cool stuff," Cooper reminded her. "With the exception of my one horrible blind date with the faeries."

"What do you think will happen next?" asked Annie.

They all thought about it for a few moments.

"We could ask the Tarot cards," Kate suggested.

"I don't think that's a good idea," Annie said. "I don't think we're supposed to know *that* much."

"I don't want to know anyway," Cooper said. "It takes all the fun out of it."

"Whatever it is, I'm sure it will be good," said Annie confidently.

"Not as good as this pie," Cooper said, looking at her plate wistfully. "Is there any more?"

Kate and Annie threw pillows at her. Cooper picked them up and threw them back. Moments later the three of them were on their feet, swinging pillows at one another and laughing so much that it hurt.

Follow the

circle of three

with Book 7: Blue Moon

Kate, Annie, and Cooper picked up the food containers and plates and took them down to the kitchen. Then Annie walked her friends to the door and said good night. Afterward she went back to her room and threw herself on the bed.

"Well, that was a lot of fun," she said aloud. "Eight o'clock on a Friday night and here I am by myself."

She was annoyed. She'd been hoping for a night of fun with her friends. A night like they usually had when they got together. But lately those nights had been few and far between. Kate and Cooper always seemed to have more important things to do. Even Annie's aunt and little sister had plans for the evening, going to a movie together so that Annie, Kate, and Cooper could have the house to themselves. But now there was no point to that. Annie was alone, and with nothing to do.

Even her plans for a blue moon ritual had been

shot down. That was something she'd been looking forward to. She'd been sure that Cooper and Kate would want to do it, too. But they didn't. They had more important things to do—things that didn't include her.

So do it yourself, she told herself. *Why do you need them?*

"Because we're a team," she said, as if she were really arguing with herself. "We're supposed to do things together. That's the whole point."

But Kate and Cooper didn't seem too worried about doing things together. They were making all kinds of plans that didn't include her. Plans with their boyfriends. Maybe it was time she started doing the same thing. *But I can't do that,* she thought. Then she paused. *Or could I?*